Also by Carissa Ann Lynch

The One Night Stand

Carissa Ann Lynch

OneMoreChapter

One More Chapter
a division of HarperCollins*Publishers*
The News Building
1 London Bridge Street
London SE1 9GF

www.harpercollins.co.uk

This paperback edition 2020

First published in Great Britain in ebook format by
HarperCollins*Publishers* 2020

A catalogue record for this book
is available from the British Library

ISBN: 978-0-00-836266-9

This novel is entirely a work of fiction.
The names, characters and incidents portrayed in it are
the work of the author's imagination. Any resemblance to
actual persons, living or dead, events or localities is
entirely coincidental.

Set in Birka by Palimpsest Book Production Ltd, Falkirk
Stirlingshire

Printed and bound in Great Britain by
CPI Group (UK) Ltd, Croydon CR0 4YY

To all the single mothers without a village

"We stopped looking for monsters under the bed when we realized they were inside us."

– Charles Darwin

Chapter 1

NOW

Wen *I think about Delaney, I think about Dillan.* Three pounds, two ounces. The delivery nurse held her out to me in the palm of her hand, like a baby bird in its mother's nest. And right on cue, my tiny fowl opened her eyes and mouth, changing my life forever.

She's alive. Delaney is going to live, I'd thought.

But in those beady black eyes, those chirpy pink lips ... I still saw the son who didn't make it: Dillan.

There's Delaney, but no Dillan.

A painful dichotomy of intense love and exceptional grief arose and gave birth to me that day.

"Only one twin survived." The doctor was soft-spoken and honey blonde; I'll never forget the contours of her face. And those words ... her words would haunt me for the next fifteen years, probably longer. There was a name for

1

my tragedy: twin-to-twin transfusion syndrome. In layman's terms, she had described it as one twin donating blood to the other. But the way she described it was almost morbid – one twin sucking up all the nutrients, sucking the life right out of its roommate ...

My beautiful Delaney was headstrong and iron-willed, and it didn't surprise me that she was the stronger of the two.

So, when I woke up to find my fifteen-year-old daughter standing over me, her eyes like shiny black marbles glowing in the moonlit shadows of my room, the first thing I thought about was Dillan.

Even now, Dillan is still one of my first thoughts each morning. I wonder what he would have looked like, as a teenager. Maybe just like Delaney, with black feathery hair and deep brown eyes. If you take away the lashes, and the girlish curve of her jaw ... I can almost see what my son would have been ...

"Mom!" Delaney hissed, tugging the blankets from my chest. It was the hiss that did it – a warning sign, that Delaney was about to scream, or in the very least, get angry and throw a few things.

"W-What is it, honey? What time is it?"

My eyes fought to stay open, my contact lenses that I wasn't supposed to sleep in at night, sticking to the backs of my eyelids.

Delaney stood up straight, her skin so pasty and pale that it was almost translucent in the low-lit room. She had this funny look on her face.

I know that look.

Not anger, which was her go-to emotion these days ... not sadness, which was probably the runner-up. No, not either of those.

Delaney is scared, I realized with a start, sitting up too fast, my head swimming as I reached for her.

"What's wrong, Laney?"

But Delaney's eyes refused to meet mine; they were trained on something else beside me ...

"There's a stranger in your bed." Her words were like shivery little whispers in the dark.

My scalp prickled with fear and I leapt from the bed, nearly knocking her backwards. I stared at the shape of a man lying on the usually empty side of my bed.

He had long legs, so long they were hanging over the end of the bed. Hairy toes poked out from beneath the blankets.

I took a small step closer, holding my breath.

He was buried beneath the sheets, except for his gangly toes and a few blond pokes of hair pricking out from the top ...

My brain tried to play catch up with what my eyes were seeing, but Delaney cut in, "Who the hell is he?" She took the words straight out of my mouth.

No longer was she that scared little girl I remembered from her youth – she had transitioned back into her usual mood: angry at times, and don't-give-a-fuck mostly.

"I have no idea, Laney."

It wasn't a lie, not exactly. I had no recollection of inviting anyone over, but it wasn't the first strange man I'd had in my bed this month ...

"Nice, Mom. Real nice," Delaney groaned.

My mind raced, thoughts trickling back to the last thing I remembered ... I'd been online again, that stupid dating site. I hadn't wanted a profile in the first place, but Pam and Jerry, my two friends from work, had set the whole thing up for me.

Did I invite one of the guys I met online to come over to the house last night? Was I drinking again? Is that why I can't remember?

Suddenly, it was starting to make sense: I rarely drank alcohol, not until recently, and not since my early twenties. If I'd had a few beers last night, or even a little wine, then maybe ... maybe I had blacked out completely.

But a quick scan of the room revealed no empty cans or bottles. No evidence that I'd been drinking at all.

How could I be so irresponsible? What the hell was I thinking, inviting a man over with my teenage daughter across the hall?

"Go back to bed. I'll wake him up and ask him to leave."

When Delaney didn't budge, I raised my voice a few octaves: "You have school in the morning. Now, go!"

The hurt expression on her face came and went so quickly, I almost wondered if I'd imagined it. A flutter of guilt rose up. Delaney wasn't a child anymore; I often had to remind myself of that. I shouldn't scold her so harshly;

4

rather, I should try to talk to her like an equal, I thought, regretfully.

"Screw you," she huffed, then turned and marched out of the room. The door to my bedroom slammed bitterly behind her.

My eyes drifted back to the lumpy man. I'd been expecting him to wake up after Laney's outburst, but he was still sleeping peacefully.

In the silence of my bedroom, I crept over to the window and sat down on my favorite reading bench that overlooked our suburban street. My head felt groggy and strange, and I waited for the details of last night to come into focus ...

I pressed my head against the windowpane and sighed. It was almost morning, the dark mountain ridges in the distance tipped with dusty browns and burgundy reds.

How long has it been since I watched the sun rise?

When Delaney was young, she'd loved the outdoors. But I had still been with her father then, Michael. Most of my memories of her early years were corrupted by memories of fights with Michael and sleepless nights as I grieved over Dillan.

Here's the thing: when you bring a baby home from the hospital, you're supposed to be happy. "It's a miracle that even one of the twins survived," the doctor had told me. "At least you have Delaney," my friends had told me.

But having a beautiful baby girl didn't make me any less sad about the son I'd lost, the room with blue borders I'd never use, the drawers of blankets and the onesies I'd picked out specifically for him ... They were all still waiting for me when I came back home from the hospital. Some things couldn't be forgotten, even if I did love Delaney with all my heart.

Michael left us when Delaney was five. Unfortunately, he didn't go far.

Less than two miles from here, he lived with his new wife, Samantha, and baby sons, Braxton and Brock, in a Victorian mansion they had restored. Delaney had a room there – she *loved* that room – and she visited them every weekend.

Apparently, Michael's not verbally abusive with his new family, and he gave up drinking years ago ... How convenient for them.

The drinking and the dating – I'd only started that recently, with the nudging insistence of my two best friends. It seemed good for me – healthy, even – but incidents like this couldn't happen.

Meeting up with strange men, bringing them to my home ... not a good example for Delaney. And probably not safe either.

I had no recollection of what had happened last night, or who this strange man was. This went way beyond normal socializing – I'd obviously blacked out completely.

I moved to another window, this one front-facing, and peered out through the blinds at the street in front of our house.

My Dodge minivan was parked at the curb, crooked as

usual. But tonight, there was a navy-blue Camaro parked behind it, and I knew it didn't belong to my neighbor. *It has to be his*, I thought, glancing back at the hairy set of toes.

Well, at least this mystery man drives a nice car. I've dated worse ...

If only I could remember who he was or what we did last night ...

"Excuse me." I tiptoed over to the bed.

I poked his shoulder area, and when he didn't budge, I pushed the blankets away from his face. His face was smooth, eyes closed. He looked downright peaceful.

Damn, I wish I slept that soundly.

"I need you to go. I don't mean to be rude, but I think I had too much to drink last night. I don't usually let guys stay overnight. And my daughter ... well, she has school in the morning. So, can you please head home?"

But the strange man didn't respond. No breathy snores, not even a slight twitch. No movement, whatsoever ...

"Excuse me!" I knew I was being a bitch, but I didn't care. My daughter had just discovered a strange man in my bed. My daughter who was already having enough troubles lately ...

Since joining the dating site, I'd invited a couple men over, but only when Delaney was at her dad's. Inviting a stranger from the internet to my house on a school night while Delaney was home ... well, that was totally out of character for me.

But lately, I hadn't been acting like myself at all.

I need this man out of my bed ... Right now.

I placed both hands on his chest and gave him a sturdy shake. "Wake up, please."

When he still didn't react, I grew frustrated. Gripping the plain white sheet in my left fist, I tugged it the rest of the way off.

"Jesus!"

I leapt back from the bed, shaky hands covering my mouth and nose.

The mystery man was completely naked, but that wasn't the shocking part. It was the dark purple stain in the center of his abdomen.

And beneath him ...

"Oh. Oh ..." The floor beneath my feet became watery and strange, the walls spinning like a tilt-o-whirl. My backside made sharp contact with the dresser behind me and a picture fell to the floor with a sickening thud.

Holding my mouth so I wouldn't scream and alert Delaney, I tiptoed like a demented ballerina, back over to the edge of the bed.

I pulled on the light string, lighting up the room to see him better.

I bit down on my fingers, muffling the terror that threatened to burst from within me ...

The stranger's face looked peaceful enough: eyes and mouth closed; hands flat at his sides. But he was rigid, *too rigid* ... almost like he was laying inside a casket instead of my bed.

It might as well be a casket ...

Because he's dead as fuck, I realized in horror.

I bit down harder, my body trembling in fear.

I moved in as close as I dared, nervously studying his wound. It was a hole above his belly button, jagged and red, with a dry purple stain blooming out like a flower around it. Dry streaks of blood stained both sides of his waist from where he'd bled out in the bed beside me.

The sheet beneath him was stained dark red with blood, so red it was almost purple.

So much blood!

It had probably soaked all the way through the mattress and box springs. There was blood on my side too. Realization sinking in, I looked down at my own blue nightdress.

No way would I have let a man see me in this old, worn-out gown. So, why am I wearing it? Nothing about this makes sense.

How the hell did he get here? And who the fuck is he?!

Tentatively, I dabbed at a big, crusty stain on the side of my gown. The color of the gown was too dark to tell, but I knew without a doubt it was blood.

His blood.

He'd been bleeding in the bed beside me ... and I'd had no idea.

Vomit tickled the back of my throat, hot and acrid.

How the hell did he get here in the first place?

And, most importantly, how did he wind up dead?

Chapter 2

NOW

Delaney had no idea that there was a dead man in my bed – not just dead, *murdered*. I'd changed my clothes, locked my bedroom door behind me, and gone to the bathroom to take a quick shower.

And when Delaney woke up at 7am for school, I was standing in the kitchen with a cup of coffee in my hands, a bowl of oatmeal and a glass of orange juice sitting on the table for her.

Most mornings were chaotic, me getting ready for work, both of us rushing out the door at the same time. But everything about today was different.

I have a feeling life will be very different from now on.

"I take it you're not going to work?" Delaney said, shuffling into the kitchen. She had on a thick black hoodie and fashionably ripped jeans, even though it was supposed to

10

be a warm day for fall. I fought the impulse to ask her to go change. She wasn't ten anymore – I couldn't pick out her clothing, as much as I would have liked to.

"I'm going in late today because I have an important meeting in the afternoon. So, my schedule is a little different." The lie flowed from my tongue like honey.

I wasn't scheduled to work late; in fact, I'd left a shaky message for my boss telling him I had a stomach virus, which isn't completely a lie.

Finding a murdered man in your bed does have the tendency to make you a little queasy ...

But I'd already missed a couple days recently; not only could I not afford another day off, but my job could be on the line.

"Right. So, ya gonna tell me who he is, or not?" Delaney demanded, globs of oatmeal swishing around her mouth as she talked. She lifted her cup of juice to her stained red lips, glanced down into the cup with a look of disgust, then slammed it back down.

I wonder what they serve for breakfast at Michael's house, I thought, drearily. Probably crepes and chocolate-chip waffles ... made from scratch by Wife #2, of course.

I took a seat in the chair across from her. "He's just a friend, honey."

My voice was so calm, so smooth ... I almost didn't recognize it.

"What—the fuck—ever." Delaney pushed the chair back with a caw-like screech, and I winced.

"Please don't talk to me that way. I'm a grown woman and I'm allowed to date if I want to. Your father has certainly moved on."

Instantly, I regretted bringing Michael and Samantha into this.

Delaney left the kitchen without another word.

I heard the jangling of her backpack slipping over her shoulders in the hall, and seconds later, the screen door thumped shut behind her. There were days when the closest I came to understanding my daughter was trying to interpret the shuffle of her feet and the velocity with which she closed her bedroom door.

I remained at the table, clutching my cup of coffee. I heard the squeaky air brakes of the bus pulling up outside. I closed my eyes, waiting for the bus to get all the way to the end of the road before I moved.

When I couldn't hear it anymore, I stood up.

Finally, I could allow myself to be shaky and afraid.

How could I be so stupid? And what am I going to do?

Obviously, I hadn't killed the man. I didn't have a violent bone in my body.

But that hasn't always been the case, has it? I scolded myself.

Is it possible? Could I have blacked out and hurt someone?

But that red-rose hole in his stomach ... It looked like a knife wound, a deep one that took a lot of strength. And anger.

I shuddered.

And if he were mentally unstable, why would he choose to take his own life in a strange woman's bed after sex, and why would he do it that way ...?

And I hadn't seen a weapon ... If he'd done it to himself, there would be a weapon ...

"Holy shit. What am I going to do?" I said aloud, the fear in my voice finally matching the terror inside me.

I carried the mug over to the kitchen sink and washed it, nearly dropping it a dozen times. Out the window above the sink, I could see my neighbor, Fran, in the street. She was fetching her mail, one arm in a cast. I waved but she didn't see me.

She had stopped, mail-in-hand, and she was staring at something. I followed her line of sight ... she was looking at the sporty blue car parked behind mine. She turned her head and looked straight at me, eyes narrowing.

"Shit, shit, shit ..."

I waited for her to turn around with her mail and wobbled back inside her own house.

The house was eerily quiet with Delaney gone, almost like a mausoleum. I wasn't used to being here during the day, and it felt wrong somehow, seeing the early morning shadows reflecting off the dusty bookshelves and cheap Ikea furniture.

Well, I guess it kind of is like a crypt, considering there's a dead man locked up in my bedroom ...

Every time I closed my eyes, each blink, each second, I could see his moon-white face, the rosy red stain on his abdomen ... the congealed blood staining my mattress and sheets.

My phone buzzed in my pocket, startling me more than it should have. I yelped, then took it out, hands quivering as I opened a new text message.

I was expecting a reply from my boss. I'd left a hoarse, whispery message for him, thankful at the time that he hadn't answered. But sooner or later, I'd have to talk to him ...

But the message was from Delaney.

I think I'll stay at Dad's again tonight. Sam and I are going to finish the library mural.
Plus, this will give you and your new friend more time together!

I could imagine her glaring out the bus window, jaw flexing in anger, her phone clutched like a weapon in her hand. Was she being nice or sarcastic?

Definitely the latter, I decided.

Every single word was like a dagger ... and I had no doubt that was her intention. She'd been angry with me every day for the past year, sometimes for a reason, but mostly not. *Teenagers are supposed to be angry, right?* I had just assumed this was normal, a part of the growing process ... but I was wrong about that. Delaney was going through a lot more than the average teen.

It was a weekday – not her dad's night to take her.

Would she explain to him why she wanted to stay with him again? What will he think about the man in my bed …?

And every time she called her stepmom *Sam*, I tasted bile in the back of my throat.

But none of this really matters right now, does it? Because I have a bigger crisis to tend to.

I knew Delaney was expecting a big reaction, for me to put up a fight …

Okay, honey. Have fun.

I typed back. I almost considered writing, 'Send Sam my love', but I knew Delaney would see right through it.

She gets her snarky humor from me, I guess.

For a split second, I could almost believe it was a normal Tuesday – dealing with Delaney's attitude and my own bitterness over Michael – but nothing about this day was normal: a murdered man was in my room.

In my bed.

Slowly, I made my way down the short, skinny hallway, breathing in through my nose and out through my mouth. I stopped in front of the bathroom door. On my tiptoes, my fingers reached for the slim, gold key that I kept on the ledge of the door frame; a master key to all the rooms in the house.

I gripped the key so tight in my right palm that it burned.

Finally, I used it to unlock my bedroom door and I stepped inside.

There was a part of me, a silly, stupid part, that hoped—*prayed*—that the body in my bed would no longer be there.

But in the light of day, the strange man still looked dead as ever.

I locked the door behind me even though I was home alone, and, noiselessly, I crept over to the bed. The sheets were hanging halfway off from where I'd tugged on them earlier. I went ahead and pulled them completely away from the bed and laid them in a crumpled pile by the door.

Shaking, I could barely breathe as I approached the naked man.

Who are you? How did you get in my bed? And most importantly, who stabbed you?

His face was wrinkle-free and hairless.

He can't be much older than thirty, I realized, finally getting a good look at him in the light of the day.

There was no jewelry on his body. No wedding ring on his finger. His fingernails and toenails were neatly trimmed, like someone who took care of himself. But, then again, not someone who would necessarily stand out from the crowd: his hair was sandy brown, his face plain, his body average ...

This man is a complete stranger to me. I've never seen him before, not a day in my life ... not on the dating site, nowhere ...

I'd been talking regularly to a few men online, but this guy wasn't one of them. New potential matches messaged daily, but I wouldn't have invited him over without at least getting to know him a little bit, would I? But then I remembered the last guy I'd had over ... I hadn't known him well either.

16

Every man I'd talked to and dated over the last month came rushing back all at once, their faces merely profile pictures, flipping one by one in my mind ...

Swipe, swipe, swipe.

And why don't I remember what happened last night?

I forced myself to move closer, to study the features of his face ...

Nearly two hours had passed since Delaney shook me awake. In that short span of time, the man's body had turned even stiffer. His eyes were still closed but his lips were parted. For a moment, I waited, expecting those lips to move, to tell me *'it's all a dream, go back to bed silly'* ...

But nothing happened.

I should call the cops.

Why hadn't I called them already?

Because it almost seems too late to do that now, a voice inside me warned.

I imagined me telling the police the truth: *I was scared. Freaked out. I didn't know what to do. So, I waited until my daughter left for school before I called you.*

No, officers, I have no idea who he is. No, I don't remember how he got here. Of course I didn't kill him! I imagined myself saying.

I couldn't call them until I could explain how he got here ... and until I could describe what transpired last night before he ended up in my bed and ended up ... dead.

But that wasn't the only reason for my hesitation. *Michael.* If he found out about this, if he found out the

17

truth about me … he would try to take Delaney away from me, permanently. He'd been doing it for years now, wearing the face of a dutiful father whenever she was around, then morphing into his old self alone with me. Nothing about the man had changed, but according to his new wife, he was perfect.

Perfect, my ass …

He wanted Delaney all to himself. That way he could have his whole, perfect family and erase me from existence completely. If he found out about this, about all of it … well, he'd probably try to get full custody for sure. Not probably – he would.

I know he would.

And the scary part: *I don't even know if Delaney would mind.*

Sure, we had our good days. But what about all the bad ones? Over the last two weeks, she'd spent more time with her other family than with me …

I imagined the cops cuffing me and carting me off to jail, Delaney sneering from the driveway, Michael smiling victoriously. And Wife #2 beside him, with her plaster-perfect smile, waving me off as they took me away …

I scurried around the room, diverting my eyes from the dead man, searching for his clothes or wallet. Something to help identify him.

I may not remember what happened, but I know I must have met him online.

A pair of dark brown chinos and a flimsy old flannel

lay messily on the floor beside my dresser. No underwear. No shoes ...?

That doesn't make sense.

I dug through the pockets of his chinos—no keys either. And no wallet.

This is insane! Did I pick up a homeless man off the street, or what?

But then I remembered the navy-blue Camaro sitting outside my house. It had to belong to him. There was no one else around it could belong to.

Rubbing my cheeks, panic surged through my veins as I tried to trace my way back in my mind ...

Did he drug me? Is that why I don't remember?

My head did feel groggy and strange, although that could be from a hangover ... And if a stranger had showed up and tried to rape me, I would have tried to defend myself. I didn't have any wounds on my hands, or the rest of my body.

And if it had been consensual sex ...

I know how my body feels after sex and this isn't it.

I wasn't sore or achy. I didn't feel violated or injured in anyway. In fact, I didn't feel like I'd had sex at all. And the old gown I'd had on when I woke up ... it was the least sexy thing I owned. I couldn't see myself putting that ratty old thing on for anyone, much less a man I'd invited over for the first time and planned to sleep with ...

I carried the man's clothes over to the pile of bedding and, shakily, dropped them to the floor. I scooped up a pair of my own jeans and a t-shirt which I'd been wearing yesterday, I remembered. The last thing I remember was fighting with Delaney.

But what happened after we fought?

She slammed her bedroom door the way she usually does, I recalled.

Then I folded laundry and made dinner. I yelled for her to come out of her room. And by the time she did, the chicken was cold. We barely ate or talked. Another silent war between us, which was all too typical for us these days – a constant battle, and one I lost more days than most.

She'd been texting furiously while she sat at the table and when I asked her who she was chatting with, she'd said, "My father", with such viciousness it had made my blood run cold.

And after dinner she'd gone back to her room and I'd gone back to mine, I remembered. On school nights, we usually went to be early, around ten or eleven or so.

But I didn't go straight to bed last night, I remembered.

I'd got online. Checked my dating profile for new messages. It was a great way to escape, and for the first time in years, I'd started feeling attractive – *wanted* – again.

I do remember getting on the site last night. But what happened after ...?

I spotted a pair of purple panties—my panties—on the floor by my side of the bed. I hated to get close to the dead guy again, but I went over to retrieve them anyway.

I gripped the underwear in a ball in my hand and forced myself to get down on my knees on the floor.

I have to check under the bed. But what if there's a knife under there? What if it's covered in blood …?

There's no such thing as monsters under the bed. I could remember saying that to Delaney countless times when she was little.

When she still needed her mother. When she still looked up to me and thought my word was gold.

Trembling, I crouched on the floor beside the bed and pressed my face to the matted carpet.

Monsters under the bed … why does that age-old fear never fully disappear with time?

I squinted into the dark, narrow gap between my bed and the floor.

I gasped and stumbled back as I came face to face with, not the murder weapon, but … another corpse.

Only this one wasn't a stranger.

Chapter 3

BEFORE

How did it begin?

I guess it started the way most bad things do: with secrets. And then, of course, there were also the lies.

Lies that tasted like malt vinegar, but flowed like syrup from our tongues ... and what was the truth anymore? I don't think we'd recognize it if it were staring us straight in the face ...

"Laney, are you ready?" I dropped my purse with a smack on the entryway floor, just like I did every day after work. I was exhausted. Most days I'd take a shower and throw together something for dinner then fall asleep watching TV.

But then I remembered: Samantha was coming.

I scooped my purse off the floor and carried the bulgy black bag to my bedroom.

Our house wasn't exactly a penthouse – paint peeling,

the original lime green from the 60s playing peek-a-boo through the cracks. But it was clean (mostly) and roomy for just the two of us. Two bedrooms, two baths. Our furniture wasn't fancy, but it was comfortable. I liked to think of our small bungalow as "homey"; it was also small enough to keep us together and large enough to keep us from killing each other ...

I kept the house tidy; well, I thought I did ... but now that I knew Samantha was coming – or *Sam* as Delaney liked to call her – the house was bathed in a whole new light.

I swept the living room curtains back, a cloud of dust tickling my nose and the back of my throat. The windows were grimy, a thin layer of dust coating the sills and every baseboard in sight.

And the air in our house ... today, it felt stale and muggy.

A pile of unpaid bills lay cluttered on the arm of the sofa from where I'd forgotten to finish sorting through them last night.

The kitchen was worse. Breakfast dishes and coffee mugs were stacked on the counter, and the drain in the sink was giving off that putrid egg smell again ...

Most days, I left for work by seven, with Delaney not far behind. There was rarely time to tidy up in the mornings, which was why I often saved all that for after work.

Leaving the dishes, I drifted back to the living room, my chest tightening with dread. In addition to the dust and messy mail pile, there were empty bottles of tea and Vitamin

Water crowding the coffee table. Delaney had been watching *Teen Mom 2* last night when I'd taken myself to bed.

When did she stop using the garbage can? I thought, angrily.

It's like you spend their early years teaching them every day common tasks and social skills, and just when you think they've mastered them, you have to re-instruct them as teens.

I stuffed the bunch of mail between two couch cushions and scooped up Delaney's mess in my arms. When I went to throw it away, I realized the garbage was full. Not only that, it smelled like last night's fettucine.

And the carpet, has it always looked this dingy?

It had been needing to be replaced since ... well, since the day we moved in nine years ago. But replacing carpet was one of those costly projects that I planned for tax return season but never got around to. Because there was always something else that came up – tires for the minivan, new school clothes for Delaney, a broken hot water heater, a busted drum in the dryer ...

It was Friday, and in our house, Fridays meant *Michael*.

Usually, Delaney's friend Viola dropped her at Michael's after school. But ever since I'd discovered the pot stash in her top drawer, Delaney had been riding the bus as part of her punishment.

I wasn't sure if her friends were bad influences, exactly, but I knew that not getting to ride with them to and from school might make Delaney think twice before picking up another joint.

Or it will make her better at hiding it, I considered, pressing down on the tender spot between my eyes and praying another migraine wasn't on its way.

I'd offered – a few times – to take Delaney to Michael's. Michael and his new wife's house was close, and it would take me less than a half hour to take her there, after work. But Samantha – or *Sam* – had insisted on picking her up this week. "It's no trouble, no trouble at all," she'd said in that high, silky voice of hers that I'd grown to detest. '*I don't work, so it's no bother. You shouldn't have to drive out here after working all day …*'

But even *that* felt like a sneaky dig – Samantha didn't work because she didn't have to. Michael's income was enough to sustain them.

Was she rubbing that in my face, or was I just being paranoid?

On the surface, Samantha seemed pleasant, polite, sweet even. But still …

No trouble at all, I thought warily, looking around at the mess I'd come home to.

"Delaney?" I shouted. Then, lowering my voice: "Are you ready in there? You should give me a hand out here."

I couldn't imagine *Sam* raising her voice, which should have made me feel better about Delaney spending so much time with her new stepmom, but there was something about her I couldn't put my finger on. Something in my gut that said she was phony.

Oh, big surprise, Ivy! You don't trust your husband's pretty new wife, the one he left you for. Join the ex-wives club, I scolded myself.

Back in my bedroom, I scraped my hair into a tight knot. I fought the urge to put on makeup.

I don't need to impress that bitch, I thought bitterly.

But I picked up a pair of tweezers and tugged on a wiry gray hair that had seemingly sprouted overnight on my right temple. My bed was still unmade from this morning, sheets and comforter tangled in a knot at the foot of the bed. I fought another urge – to crawl under the covers and live there.

Maybe I'll hide in here when she knocks, I considered. *Nobody's home …*

I left the room and closed the door behind me.

I'll deal with that mess later, I decided.

I shuffled down the dimly lit hallway. There was still no sign of Delaney.

I stopped in front of the bathroom and pressed my ear to the door. Water was running, and I could hear something else – the faint sound of Delaney humming while she took a shower. Ever since Delaney had started high school, she had started taking extra-long showers.

Her sweet, melancholic voice was indistinguishable from that of a child's. For a moment, I could almost believe that on the other side of this door was my daughter, my old daughter, the one who splashed and sang, who squealed for me to jump in the tub and join her.

No, that daughter had been replaced with a new one

– the daughter who locks every door and sneaks stashes of pot into her bedroom drawers ...

I rapped softly on the door, but didn't bother turning the knob – she always locked every single door behind her.

So secretive ... but that's the way of teenagers, isn't it? There's always some vulnerable, wounded part of themselves they feel like they have to tuck away and hide. The person they trust the most as a child becomes the last person on Earth they'd ever confide in ...

The humming stopped for a split second, but then it started up again.

Ignoring me, as usual.

The tune she was humming sounded familiar.

Row, row, row your boat ...

"Delaney." I knocked again, harder this time. "You need to finish up. Samantha's due here any minute. It's rude to be in the shower when you know someone is on their way to pick you up ..."

I didn't wait for an answer because I knew there wouldn't be one.

Truth was, I was less worried about Delaney's rudeness than my discomfort with the idea of being stuck interacting with *Sam* while Delaney got her shit together.

I'd imagined this whole pick-up going more smoothly— Delaney standing by the front door with her backpack in hand and ready, the exchange between Sam and I polite, but brisk. *Very brisk.* Then I'd stand on the front porch and wave. "Have a good time, you two!" I imagined myself shouting, in that perfect, *non-jealous* way, that responsible co-parents do.

But that scenario wasn't going to happen.

Michael nor Samantha had been to our house in a couple years; the drop-offs and pick-ups always facilitated by me, or Delaney's friends. And I liked it that way—the last thing I needed was Michael's judgement—his eyes scanning every square inch of our small modest home.

At least it's Samantha coming, not him. But still … I don't feel like I can trust her either. I always feel like I'm under a microscope, being judged.

It's a strange feeling, being watched and overlooked at the same time …

My feet were achy from work, but I refrained from kicking off my dress flats; instead, I got busy washing the sticky mugs from this morning, and I hauled the garbage out to the dumpster in the alley out back.

By the time my lovely daughter emerged from the bathroom, the kitchen was neat and organized, and I was working the vacuum back and forth over the carpet in the living room, humming a mindless tune of my own.

Samantha was late, which surprised me a little, but also came as a relief.

The house is looking pretty good now, if I must say so myself …

But when I looked up and saw my daughter's face, my insides turned cold. Delaney was gripping her cell phone in her hand, shaking like a leaf.

I kicked the vacuum off with my right foot and pulled the cord from the wall.

"What's going on?"

Delaney was wearing skin-tight maroon leggings with a stretchy black blouse. I'd never seen the outfit before – undoubtedly, a new gift from her father or stepmom. My daughter was painfully pretty, in that way all young people are, skin soft and youthful like putty. Her body and face undamaged by motherhood, or time. You'd think I'd be used to it by now, but even after fifteen years, the depth of my daughter's beauty always knocked me off guard.

People say we look alike, but I don't see it.

And she was wearing makeup, something new – a silky slip of gloss on her lips, reddish-brown shadow a strange contrast with her navy-blue eyes. However, her long black hair was still tangled and damp from the shower.

Something was wrong; there was a milky-white shade to her skin, and she was gnawing on her bottom lip, the way she used to do when she was young ...

"Well, what is it? What's wrong?" I tried to suppress my annoyance. Another thing about Delaney since becoming a teenager: she was dramatic as hell and getting an answer out of her was like pulling teeth with a pair of chopsticks.

"It's Sam. There ... well, there's been an accident."

And just like that, Delaney's woman-like façade crumbled completely. Her nose wrinkled up and she reached

29

for me, falling into my chest. I held her there, shock rolling through me.

Delaney was sobbing, her body rocking back and forth into mine.

"Oh my gosh. What kind of accident?" I whispered.

I rubbed her back in slow circles, soothing her at my breast, just as I had done when she was young and needed me. But this felt different, and for the life of me, I couldn't remember the last time I'd held her.

It's been years, I realized sullenly.

As I hugged her, I could feel her bones through her skin, no more baby fat. Overnight, she'd become sharp angles and blunt curves ... a total stranger to me.

When did she lose weight? And why haven't I noticed before now?

Delaney still hadn't answered. I felt desperate to know, but my heart ached as she shook and cried in my arms.

Could my husband's new wife be ... dead?

For a brief moment, I considered how that would make me feel, *really feel*. Sure, I resented Samantha, but dead?

No, I wouldn't wish that on anybody. Especially not someone my daughter's grown so fond of. Her happiness is more important than any resentment I feel toward Michael and Samantha.

But there was another part of me, that niggly fierce mother in me, that felt slightly pained by my daughter's strong reaction.

It must be bad.

"Shhh ... I'm sure it will be okay." I stroked the top of Delaney's hair, breathing in the heady smell of her honey-scented shampoo.

Delaney pulled back with a surprised jerk, flustered. She wiped her face with the back of her hands, smoothed her rumpled hair into place.

She remembers who she is now. No longer a baby who cries in her mother's arms ...

"Dad texted while I was in the shower. Sam was on the way to get me when someone ran a red light and hit the side of her Mercedes. She's being taken to University Hospital. Her neck is broken, and some other things ... That's all I know."

"Oh my God, that sounds serious," I said, reaching for her. I wanted to hold her again, try to make it better ... but, this time, she side-stepped me. With her back pressed to the couch, Delaney took out her cell phone out and started punching keys. "I need to go to the hospital. I need to make sure she's okay. And Dad probably needs me too. He sounded very worried ..."

"Yes, of course, we should go right now. Let me grab my purse and slide on my shoes, then I'll take you."

Moments later, we were buckling our seatbelts in the minivan and backing out of the driveway. Delaney twisted her hair into a tight, wet knot at the base of her skull that oddly resembled my own.

"I know you must be so worried, honey. Are you okay?" I reached over out of habit, ready to pat her knee.

"I'm fine," she snapped, inching her legs out of reach. She shifted her body towards the passenger's window, still struggling to smooth the frizzy, loose pieces of hair that poked out from the stubby bun.

Twenty minutes later, the glaring red lights of University Hospital came into view. I flicked my signal on and turned into the crowded lot.

"I'll park in the garage. We can take the elevator up—"

"No, just drop me in the front."

I tapped my brakes outside the emergency room entrance, hesitating.

"But we could get towed. It'll only take a moment to grab a spot, Laney. I'll be fast, I promise."

"Mom," Delaney whined, "just drop me in the front, okay? I'll call you in a little while with an update."

"Oh." I felt my cheeks growing warm. "You don't want me to come inside with you? I'm sure your dad wouldn't mind. I'm concerned for Samantha too ..."

"The last thing Dad needs is an extra stressor, okay? I'll let you know how she's doing as soon as I can. And I think you're right; she's going to be okay."

"Yes, I'm sure she will," I said, still hearing the ring of that word 'stressor' in my ears.

Is that all I am to my ex now, an extra blip of stress in his busy radar of life?

I parked at the curb behind a row of flashing ambulances. I watched two paramedics, as they unloaded an elderly man out the back on a big, white gurney.

Delaney let herself out the passenger's side, not looking back or saying goodbye. I watched my daughter as she ran towards the entrance, joining up with two familiar faces at the door: my ex-sister-in-law, Fiona, and my ex-father-in-law, Joseph.

Glad to see they turned out for Samantha. They didn't even come to the hospital when Delaney and Dillan were born …

My face burned with shame.

I shouldn't be thinking of myself at a time like this. Samantha has been injured and my daughter's upset.

Joseph and Fiona glanced over at me, expressions stony. Then, pretending I didn't exist the way they always did, they looked away. I watched as Joseph wrapped a thick arm around Delaney's shoulders and led her inside the hospital. I waited for them to disappear through the revolving doors.

The sun was nearly gone, the sky an ominous indigo color. I made the slow drive home, not even bothering with the radio.

As I approached our subdivision, I flicked my high beams on to combat the fog. My thoughts were muddled and strange.

Will Samantha be okay? What if she's not? Will Delaney be alright? But then those questions swelled into darker ones: *Why is Delaney so distraught over her stepmom? And why is she always so impressed by her? Am I losing my daughter completely? And why am I so damned jealous?*

I could see it in Delaney's eyes when she talked about

33

her stepmom – they lit up. '*Sam's such a talented painter. Sam has a moon and star tattoo on her back. Sam showed me how to mix paint properly …*'

Blah blah fucking blah.

But guilt fluttered back.

This is no time for being petty.

I wasn't normally the praying type, but I said a small prayer under my breath for Samantha.

When I pulled in, there was a red Miata parked in my driveway. Loud 90s rap music boomed from the speakers, seemingly shaking the entire block.

Good thing I only have one neighbor for miles.

I parked beside the Miata, smiling warily.

"There you are!" Pam squealed. My oldest friend – my *best* friend – was sitting in the driver's seat, blonde hair crispy with hairspray. When she smiled, I saw a smudge of bright red lipstick on her freshly whitened teeth. I motioned for her to turn down the radio.

"Sorry," she said, grinning wildly. But her manic smile evaporated when she saw the worried look on my face. I rolled my window down farther, then turned off the engine.

"Oh, Ivy. What's the matter?"

Unhooking my seatbelt, I leaned my seat back a little and took a deep breath.

There's something about being around my best friend that makes me want to lie down and relax, tell her all about my day like she's Sigmund Freud …

"Samantha had an accident on her way to pick up

Delaney. She's at the hospital. It's serious, apparently. She has a broken neck."

Pam's eyes widened. "And we're upset about this, right?"

"Fuck, Pam. Of course we are. Delaney's upset. They've gotten so close ..."

Pam raised her eyebrows, in that *Are you okay with that?* sort of way I found annoying.

That's the bad thing about best friends: they always know the things you think but cannot say. And Pam knew my secrets better than anyone.

"I'm sure she'll be okay, but Laney was so upset. I just hope they're all okay. What are you doing here, anyway? Not that I'm not glad to see you ..."

Pam and I worked together, but Fridays were usually her day off.

"I came to pick you up, silly. Did you really think I'd let you spend your birthday alone?" Pam patted the empty passenger's seat with a sly grin.

My birthday.

I'd nearly forgotten about it since this morning, not that birthdays were a big deal for me anymore. The fact that Delaney hadn't wished me happy birthday all day had hurt a little, but maybe she had been going to, until Samantha's accident?

When Delaney was little, she'd loved birthdays – the cake and the candles, the singing and the presents. Hell, even when it wasn't one of our birthdays, she'd hold pretend birthday parties with her dolls and stuffed animals. One year, I'd even bought her a big plastic cake to play with at Christmas ...

"You're so sweet, but I can't go anywhere. I need to stick around in case Laney needs me. She might want me to come to the hospital ..."

"Ivy," Pam said, sternly, "it's Michael's day to take care of her, and I'm sure she'll call you if she needs you. She's a big girl now, and we won't go far. Just down to the pub for dinner and drinks. Jerry's meeting us there, too."

"I'm still in my damn work clothes," I grunted, pointing at my faded green polo shirt.

Pam gave me a look.

I know that look.

She wouldn't take no for an answer.

"Okay, fine. At least let me go change real quick. But is it okay if I follow you down there instead of riding?" Pam was a heavy drinker at times – never a drunk – but she often drank a few too many when she went out. And lately, she went out a lot more than I did.

We hadn't gone "out" together in a long time, and I just felt safer driving myself.

"Just in case Laney calls while we're out. I want to be able to go and get her if I need to," I explained.

"Fine," Pam groaned, waving for me to hurry up and get ready.

Dinner and drinks with Pam and Jerry, my two best friends – my *only* friends, really – sounded pretty good, actually.

Hell, you only turn forty once, right?

"I'll wait out here," Pam croaked, lighting a cigarette and blowing a big cloud of smoke in my direction. By the time I had my front door open, her music was blasting again.

The living room was dark, and I nearly tripped over the vacuum I'd left out earlier.

It took me a few minutes to pick out something to wear. Finally, I settled on a black pencil skirt and a silky red and black top that was getting tight around my waistline but still hugged my breasts just right. Then I combed my hair and brushed my teeth, strutting back outside. I forced myself to smile with all my teeth – mostly for Pam's benefit, but also in the hopes it would lift my own sour mood.

Pam was smoking another cigarette, looking down at the pink iPhone in her lap.

"Look okay?" I did a goofy spin in the driveway. Suddenly, the idea of being with Jerry and Pam instead of at home worrying by myself *did* sound kind of fun.

"You're gorgeous, Ivy. Don't look a day over thirty!" she teased.

"Oh, bullshit. But thanks. I'll be right behind you, but first, let me text Laney. I want to see how she's doing, see if she has any updates on Sam."

"Sam. When did you start calling her that?" Pam snorted.

I waved dismissively and took my phone out of my purse.

I was a little disappointed to see that Delaney hadn't messaged me with any news yet, but it had only been a half hour since I'd dropped her off.

I typed:

How is Sam doing? Call me if you need me and I'll be right there.

As soon as I clicked send, I heard a tiny ding coming from the passenger's side floorboard.

I was surprised to see Delaney's phone, a black Android with a bedazzled case lying face down on the floor.

She must have dropped it when she got out earlier …

Delaney guarded her phone like a precious jewel. Not uncommon for any teen, I guess.

I could remember tucking my pager away, hiding it between my mattress and box spring, but I'm not exactly sure who I was hiding it from since my parents were already dead by then …

I stared at the phone, sparkling in the hazy moonlight outside my window.

It wouldn't take Delaney long before she realized she'd left her phone behind, if she hadn't already.

Pam honked beside me and I yelped.

"Alright. Let's go," I groaned, shifting the van into gear.

***

My hands were clammy on the steering wheel as I squeezed between a truck and a Volvo in the back row of Midge's Bar and Grill. It was "our" spot – Pam, Jerry, and me – on those rare days when we were granted an extended lunch break. They had excellent salads and pasta bowls for lunch, but I'd never been here this late at night.

The parking lot was crowded with cars and the screeching sound of an electric guitar floated from the open deck that was normally closed in the daytime. Couples and groups were wandering through the parking lot, making their way inside.

I gave Delaney's phone on the floor one last, longing glance, then I took out my own phone and messaged Michael.

Delaney left her phone in the van. I thought she might be looking for it. If she needs me, will you have her give me a call from your cell, please?

I clicked send, then added one more text:

Wishing and praying for Samantha.

Reading it back, it looked corny. And maybe a little sarcastic. Would Michael believe me?

Probably not, I decided.

There was no love lost between us – well, not anymore. He knew I was angry and resentful, and I knew he didn't give a shit. He'd never apologized for cheating on me, not even once …

As I shimmied out of the van, I couldn't help noticing that everyone looked much younger, much prettier.

Is this what it feels like to get old?

A tiny knot of women – well, girls, really – slid past me, cell phones held out in front of their faces, giggling. They were all wearing high-waisted jeans and trendy crop tops that they must have coordinated beforehand.

"Makes you feel old, don't it?" Pam teased, bumping her hip up against mine.

"Nah. Just wiser," I said, adjusting my purse across my chest and settling it on my right hip. I clicked the automatic lock button on my key fob. "And it's too damn cold for tube tops anyway."

As we approached the glowing orange lights of the restaurant entrance, I immediately spotted Jerry standing out front. His hands were tucked in his jean pockets. The gaggle of pretty girls went by, but he didn't seem to notice.

Jerry had a face like a ham hock, sweaty and pink. He's definitely not what I'd call handsome, but his close-set brown eyes were kind, and his mischievous, joker-like smile was undoubtedly his most attractive feature. The three of us had been friends for nearly a decade now, working together at the same marketing firm.

For the longest time, I thought Jerry and Pam had a "thing", but she had assured me it was never like that. If Jerry dated, Pam and I didn't know about it. He seemed perfectly content with being single.

"Happy birthday, love," Jerry scooped me into a hug, lifting my feet off the ground as he did so.

"Oh, wow. Someone's excited tonight," Pam teased.

"Thanks, Jerry," I said, adjusting my skirt as he dropped me back down on the pavement.

"I saw you this morning, remember? He already wished me a happy birthday like fifty times," I told Pam.

"Yeah, but you know how it is. Nothing at work feels real. Now we can really celebrate. The big four-oh! It's supposed to be a big one, you know ..." Jerry held open the entrance door for Pam and me.

"I can't stay long," I tried to tell them, but I was hit with a blast of live music and people chattering. Trying to talk now was like screaming into a deep dark void.

Jerry pointed through the crowd at an open table near the bar, but away from the band, and Pam and I led the way.

"Wow. I can't believe this place gets so crowded. Definitely different than the lunch crowd," I shouted, taking a seat at the four-person table. I hopped up on one of the stools and tried to scoot in closer to the table. The seats were so high that my feet dangled several inches from the ground.

"So, what did you and Delaney do for your birthday? Anything?" Jerry asked, leaning in, his expression hopeful. He was sitting across from me, Pam at his elbow. They were sitting so close to one another, and, once again, it crossed my mind that they were a couple. If not, maybe they should be ...

"No, nothing. Although we wouldn't have had time to anyway." I brought him up to speed on what had happened to Samantha.

Our waitress swooped in, taking our drink order.

"Serves her right," Jerry mumbled under his breath. He adjusted the sugar packets on the table and rearranged the bottles of ketchup and steak sauce.

41

"Jerry don't say that," Pam slapped his arm and widened her eyes at me.

"Well, it's true. She stole Ivy's husband. You can't shit on people like that and expect karma not to rear up sooner or later ..."

My mind wandered back to the day Michael had told me '*I've met someone. I think you and I both know it's for the best ...*' He was no nonchalant when he said it and I instantly felt too foolish to speak the truth – that I *was* shocked. In fact, I felt completely blindsided by it.

I'd thought things were okay between us, better than okay, actually.

The waitress returned with a tray full of drinks. She placed our drinks neatly in front of us on matching coasters. An amaretto sour for me. Dark Belgian beers for Jerry and Pam.

We clinked our glasses together jovially, then I took a long swig of mine. My cheeks puckered and I set the drink back down on the table.

"First of all, nobody *stole* Michael from me. He chose to go on his own. And although I'm not crazy about Samantha, Laney is. She likes her, and right now, Laney doesn't like much of anyone. So, I can't, in good conscience, ever wish ill of Michael's wife."

Pam and Jerry exchanged looks, clearly impressed.

I must admit, I was impressed myself.

I sat up straighter and took another sip of the acidic drink.

I meant what I said. I don't want anything bad to happen to Laney's stepmom. But a few years ago, that wouldn't have been the case.

"I'm proud of you. You've really turned over a new leaf, my friend." Pam reached across the table and squeezed my hand. The gesture was kind and I was surprised to feel my eyes watering uncontrollably.

Jerry tapped my toe under the table and smiled. Just like that, I felt my shoulders loosen, the tension in my stomach easing.

It's my birthday. And I have two awesome friends here with me. Hell, I might be forty and I might be divorced, but I like my job and I love my friends. And most importantly, I still have Laney, even if she's going through a rebellious teenage phase …

"Speaking of new leaves, Pam and I have something to tell you," Jerry said, out of the blue.

I watched my two best friends exchange smirky little smiles again.

Were they finally going to admit that they were dating?

"Well, come on then. Spill those guts," I teased, sloshing the ice around in my drink with a straw. I could already feel a smidge of heartburn rising from my stomach.

"We sort of … well, we did a thing. For your birthday, Ivy," Pam grimaced.

"Oh?" I said, slightly disappointed.

I'm not a fan of gifts or big displays of affection.

Jerry and Pam knew that better than anyone.

Jerry took out his shiny black Android, flashed another

knowing smile at Pam, then set his phone down on the table. He clicked the home button and slid it across the table toward me.

I stared at the screen and blinked. My own face peered back at me.

"What is this?"

I recognized the picture: me, in a slim-fitting cocktail dress, cleavage propped up more than usual. Pam had taken the photo at last year's Christmas party; it was one of those rare pictures that turned out well only because I wasn't trying too hard to smile, or to get the right angle. She'd sent it to me last year, encouraging me to use it as my profile pic on Facebook. I had considered it, but ultimately, decided not to. I looked too carefree and silly in the photo.

"Scroll down." Jerry tapped his pointer finger on the table, excitedly. He looked all too pleased with himself.

A flicker of irritation rolled through me.

What the hell had they gone and done now?

I did what he said and scrolled.

Ivy, 30, from Madison, Indiana

Likes: camping trips, boating, scary movies, thriller novels

"Camping? Thriller novels? What the hell is this, guys? And you put my age down as 30! Why?" I was laughing, but my face felt hot.

My best friends set me up a dating profile! It doesn't get more pathetic than that …

"You can change it up any way you'd like. It's not live

yet, so don't be mad. We just thought it'd be good for you, ya know? You're kind and funny, not to mention smoking hot ... and you deserve to have some fun," Pam gushed. She scanned my face, waiting for my approval.

"You guys suck, you know that?" I covered my face with my hands, rubbing them up and down.

"Here's the log-in information and password. You can change anything you'd like. We added some more stuff about you, too ... and there are two more pictures on there." Jerry passed me a yellow sticky note with the words IvyGirl807 and 35818 written on it in his sloppy scrawl.

I snatched the note up and jammed it inside the purse on the stool beside me.

Our waitress had reappeared, this time with a steaming white plate of mussels.

"Ooh, that's a great picture of you," she crooned, wiggling her brows at the photo displayed on Jerry's phone.

My cheeks flushed and I flipped the phone over on the table.

"Thanks," I said, quietly.

"There are so many attractive guys on there. And girls too! Promise me you'll check it out," Pam whined, slamming back her second beer and shouting after the waitress for a third.

"I will," I lied, fingers grasping one of the mussel shells. "So, how was your day off?" I tried to change the subject, uncomfortable with this intense focus on me and my lackluster love life.

I sucked the flesh from the shell while Pam told Jerry and me about her two intakes at the shelter today—an abused labrador and a lost Balinese kitten. She had been volunteering at the local animal shelter every Friday and Saturday for years now, and though she was one of those people who viewed animals as children, she never brought any home with her from work.

Oh, how nice it would be to have a sassy pup instead of a rabid teen in my house ...

I was grateful to have a change in topic. I listened to my friends talk, but I didn't hear much of what they said because I was slightly irritated about the whole dating site thing.

Who the fuck do they think they are setting that up without asking me? Am I that desperate in their eyes?

I tried to imagine the conversation that must have taken place between them when they decided to set it up. Pam saying, *'Poor Ivy. You know what she really needs for her birthday? A man!'*

Pam was single too, but she dated regularly, either guys she met on dating sites or blokes she met in bars. Unlike me, she had never been married.

I was also still worried about Delaney and Samantha. I checked my phone for the hundredth time but Michael had not responded to my texts.

Surely, if Delaney needed me, she would get a hold of me, I assured myself.

"Helloooo," Jerry said, breaking into my thoughts with the snap of his fingers.

"What?" I snapped. "Sorry. Just thinking about Delaney again ..."

"Well, we're trying to get your mind off that. Where should we go next? You're the birthday girl, you decide."

"Next?" I took a sip of my drink. By now, the amaretto sour was lukewarm, and the mussels were swishing around in my belly. All I wanted to do was go back home and fall asleep early.

Damn, maybe I am getting old.

"Yeah, I thought we could go out to a club. There are some new ones that just opened over in Kentucky. Maybe have some more drinks, do a little dancing like the old days? And before you say no, don't worry. Jerry will be the DD if we need him," Pam pleaded.

The words "no" and "I'm tired" floated on the tip of my tongue. And they wouldn't have been a lie – I was tired. And stressed out.

I want to go home, crawl into bed, and sleep.

But my mind wandered back to the dating profile, that giddy, carefree version of me in that profile pic. And my friends, so desperate to see me dating again. Maybe it wasn't a terrible idea, but it still made me nervous just thinking about it. The last man I was with was Michael, and ... well, look how that turned out.

"Okay, I'll go ... but only for a little while. I need to get home in case—"

"We know, we know. In case Delaney needs you," Jerry said, laughing.

Pam and Jerry were kind enough to settle the bill, covering my part of the food and my drink for my birthday. As we walked outside, I was hit with a vague memory: stumbling out of a restaurant just like this one ... only then, it had been my twenty-first birthday. Michael clutching my arm for support. We were both drunk, completely unfit to be driving. But we didn't care – we were so in love, or lust, that all we could think about was getting back to his apartment, getting each other alone ...

'I can't wait to get you back to my place. Give you some birthday dessert, baby,' he'd purred in my ear. He flicked my lobe with his tongue. It was cheesy – all of it – but his words created tingly shocks of pleasure that started on my scalp and trickled all the way to my toes.

Michael, always the charmer. Until he wasn't.

"Listen, I'm going to follow you there," I said, opening the door of the van. I expected more protests and was relieved when they didn't.

It had been so long since I'd been to Grisham Boulevard, which was where most of the popular bars and night clubs were in Kentucky.

"You sure you don't want to ride with me now? You could leave your car here till morning," Jerry stood outside the driver's window, jingling his keys. Pam was clutching his arm, clearly too drunk to drive herself after those four beers.

"Nah, that's okay. I'll park in the garage by Grisham, and then if I need you to take me home, at least I'll know the van is safely parked."

In reality, I wasn't planning on having any more drinks. The amaretto sour had hurt my belly and left a terrible aftertaste in the back of my mouth.

Plus, I wanted to be able to drive home so I didn't have to deal with tracking down my van in the morning. Too many days in my youth had been spent recuperating from the night before ...

I placed my purse on the passenger seat and tugged my driver's mirror down to check for food in my teeth.

Even now, I'm shocked by the woman looking back at me.

I guess I was still expecting that younger version, the one with the smooth white skin and shiny black hair minus the wiry gray strands, the girl with the killer smile and the confidence to back it up. Once upon a time, I could turn heads. Including Michael's.

But I don't turn heads anymore.

Maybe the dating app isn't such a bad idea, I considered.

Pam had shared a few stories about her dating escapades with me. Was I impressed?

No, not really. I sort of felt sorry for her.

My mind drifted back to Delaney, as I waited for Jerry to pull up beside me so I could follow him there.

The phone on the floorboard chirped again. I'd nearly forgotten about it, lying down there in the dark. Grunting, I reached across the seat and scooped it up.

Delaney will definitely be wanting this back in the morning, I thought, furtively.

I stared at the screen of her iPhone. The screen saver

was a picture of her and her best friend, Kerry. Kerry was all smiles and puckered lips, but Delaney ... she frowned into the lens, her eyes narrowed and intense. She looked almost ... *angry*. And everything about the photo screamed: '*Don't fuck with me.*'

Maybe that's exactly what she was aiming for, I considered.

I swiped right, mostly to erase that vexed image of her, and was instantly met with a prompt to put in a password. Without thinking I punched in the six-digit code Delaney and I had both been using for years now, the one she used to use for Roblox and other online kid games. But that had been years ago; surely, she had changed it by now?

Surprisingly, the password still worked. Like me, Delaney was a creature of habit.

A dozen app icons filled the screen. I was relieved to see that her wallpaper was a simple design, blue ocean water and steamy white caps on a stranded beach. It felt wrong looking at her phone like this. And if Delaney knew I was snooping, there would be hell to pay.

She would be livid, no doubt.

But isn't this what responsible parents are supposed to do? Check up on their teens?

My mother was dead by the time I was Delaney's age, and I could have used one with all the trouble I got into.

Delaney had two unread text messages blinking back at me in the corner. Before I could change my mind, I clicked on the message app.

The first one was the message I'd sent her earlier, telling her to call me if she needed me.

And the newest one ... I clicked on it and waited for an image to load on the screen.

My mouth fell open and I released a small cry, covering my mouth in horror.

"What're ya doing over there? Let's go!" Pam shouted from Jerry's passenger window. They were parked right in front of me, blinding white headlights shining in my eyes.

I quickly pressed the home button and the screen went dark. Shaking, I reached over for my purse and buried the phone deep inside.

I rolled my window all the way down, leaned out, then shouted, "I'm so sorry, but I have to go now. Delaney needs me at the hospital. Thanks for dinner. We'll do it again soon, yeah?"

"Yeah, of course," Pam said, but I could tell she didn't believe me. She slumped back in her seat, and I could see she was already texting away on her phone.

If Jerry and I are here, then who is she texting? I wondered.

Pam didn't have any other close friends, but she was friendly with a lot of people ...

But it didn't matter – my thoughts were with Delaney now.

The image on my daughter's phone flashed in my mind again. Repulsed, I shook my head, willing it to go away. Jerry honked and waved, then I watched their taillights disappear from the restaurant parking lot. Finally, I put the van in gear and started the slow crawl home.

Chapter 4

BEFORE

The house was cloaked in a dark cloud, not a single light on inside or outside, since I'd left them all off when I'd gone out for my birthday.

Oak Hill was not only a subdivision, but a *community*. At least that was what the original advertisement had claimed. I had one neighbor across the street; both houses beside me – near replicas of mine – lay neglected and empty.

Almost all the houses in Oak Hill were empty. The clubhouse and the pool that they boasted about building years ago ... well, those never happened. The people and the houses in the brochure were sunshiny, gleaming with community, with joy and a stark contrast to the somber reality I came home to every day.

A perfect house in theory; but a lonely, empty place in truth.

It was like living in our own little ghost town, which at first, when we moved in, we thought was neat. I never had to worry about Delaney riding her bike outside, but then again, there was no one for her to play with either. And as the years marched on, the whole subdivision felt deserted and a little depressing.

At least we have Fran across the street, I thought, rolling my eyes.

Fran looked to be around seventy years old and, according to Pam's sources, she was widowed. Although she rarely left the house, she was always watching, peeking through the blinds as we came or went, goggling at us when she fetched her mail. And although I'd tried being neighborly, waving and smiling, she was never friendly back, almost pretending like she didn't see us at all.

Finally, after the first year of living here, I stopped waving completely.

Maybe she's senile, I had considered. *Or maybe her vision's gone bad.*

Or maybe she doesn't like having neighbors, period.

Tonight, her house was as dark as ours, giving the entire neighborhood the hush of an overgrown, forgotten cemetery. The empty houses were like looming headstones, a reminder of what could have been.

I wonder where Fran is. She's usually home, every night …

Hell, maybe Fran is out on a date. I wouldn't be surprised if her love life was better than mine, I thought, glumly.

I locked the van, then followed the stony pathway up

to my front door. I let myself in, clicking the door locked behind me and slammed into something tall and hard, yelping in pain.

"Damn you!" I kicked the vacuum cleaner on its side, then stopped myself and took a breath.

It's going to be okay. Just stay calm, Ivy.

Room by room I went, flooding the house with lights. The house came alive, instantly making me feel better, and more in control. I imagined how it would look from space, one glowing bulb in the center of a pitch-black ghost land.

I shimmied out of my pencil skirt and too-tight blouse, then tugged on my favorite sweats and a raggedy old Bengals t-shirt.

I hardly ever drank, but that amaretto had got me going, so I tracked down an old bottle of Moscato in the back of the fridge, then slid out a dusty old wine glass from the cupboard.

I blew the dust off and poured, sighing as I did so.

What am I going to do with that daughter of mine?

The image on her phone came rushing back ...

I tipped the glass back, eager to taste the sweet cherry fizz.

I swallowed, slowly, then squinted into the glass.

What the hell?

Just to be sure, I took a few more sips.

Yep. No doubt. This is water, not wine.

So, Laney was drinking. Enough to know that she had to cover her tracks by switching out the nearly forgotten bottle in the back of the fridge. Add that to my growing list of concerns.

I turned the bottle on its side over the sink basin, watching as the long, slow stream chugged down the drain in splashy waves.

Laney is drinking. But that is small potatoes compared to what I found on her phone.

Angrily, I launched the bottle across the room. It landed with a hard clank on the floor beside the trash, but it didn't break.

Go figure.

I only tear up things I want to fix. Never the other way around anymore.

I stomped towards my daughter's room. Her door was closed, which wasn't unusual. Delaney was all about her privacy these days.

Finally, I understand why.

Weekends were the only time I was home alone in the house. I'd considered snooping in the past, but there was something about it that always made me uneasy, guilty, for not allowing her this one safe space she could call her own.

And how would I feel if she was snooping through my room?

But in reality, how smart is it to give her so much space and privacy?

I wasn't sure anymore.

Not very smart, apparently.

The light was off in her room. I flipped it on, giving

my eyes a few seconds to adjust. I rarely saw the place anymore. Delaney slipped in and out like a phantom – a flash in the morning, a blip at the dinner table, a quiet little mouse at bedtime ...

It had been so long since I'd been in her room that I'd nearly forgotten what it looked like.

I was surprised to find it neat and organized. The bed was made; the same fuzzy blue blanket with little curls of lace was tucked stiffly in each corner.

Bob, the stuffed elephant, was perched in the center of her pillows.

My heart swelled at the sight of him. I sank down on the bed, the springs squeaky and old, and I reached for the frumpy old toy. His short gray hair was coarser than I remembered – it used to feel so soft and smooth on my fingertips. I could remember packing Bob in the car and in her night bag on trips to Michael's, because Delaney couldn't go without him.

Now, his fur felt stiff and matted. He'd gotten old. Just like me. Just like Delaney ... She's not a smooth little girl anymore; she's coarser, rougher around the edges ...

She's keeping a secret.

I took her phone out of my pocket and clicked the home screen. Taking a deep breath, I clicked on the messages again. It felt wrong – so damn wrong – looking at this image.

It was a picture of a naked boy.

A boy, or was it a man?

It was impossible to know for sure because his head and neck were missing. Only the space between his chest and thighs was exposed.

He gripped his penis in his hand, crudely.

It was hard to discern his age; he had some hair on his chest and the rest of his body, but there was really no way to tell. Was this a teenage boy my daughter hadn't told me about? Or was this someone else ... a predator? A stranger?

My mom brain was spinning out of control ...

Luckily, from what I could tell, Delaney hadn't sent any of her own pictures.

But who knew what she had erased?

If she is sending pictures of herself, oh my God ... What if this boy became angry and shared naked pictures of her all over school? Or worse, all over the internet?

There were no words exchanged, only the one picture. And it came from a number without a name, someone she didn't keep in her address book.

No name, no face, his identity a complete mystery.

I scanned through the rest of Delaney's messages, the guilt I'd felt earlier temporarily forgotten.

I saw messages from Michael and a few from Samantha. Messages from me. But other than that, there were no messages from her school friends.

Has she erased some of them? She must have, I decided.

The internet history on her cell phone showed no results. I wasn't so old that I didn't understand what this meant:

Delaney had either deleted her search history, or she was using in-private browsing.

No photos either – possibly stored on iCloud? I considered.

Besides the photo messages from the mystery man/boy, there was nothing suspect on her phone. I shut it off and stood up, placing it face down on her dresser.

Her dresser was neat, brushes and combs lined up evenly. An open makeup bag in the middle. I picked through it, fingers brushing over the new reddish-brown shadow I'd seen on her earlier. My heart ached.

I want my daughter back.

I stared at my own face in the mirror. My black hair was turning gray; the wrinkles on my forehead and between my brows were deepening by the day.

Worries like these probably don't help with wrinkles either.

I imagined Delaney standing in this exact same spot, staring at herself every day in the mirror. She was beautiful, in that way that's almost grotesque. Too perfect. Too unflawed. But she'd lost weight.

Was she self-conscious? Was she hurting more than I realized?

Monstrous beauty can seem like a blessing, but it's also a curse. Sometimes the monsters don't know how powerful their beauty is ...

So, what if she's exchanging sexy pics with a boy? Is this really as big a deal as I think it is?

Wasn't I doing the exact same thing at her age? I considered. No, I wasn't. Not because I wouldn't have, but because I was so busy grieving the loss of my parents after their car accident, and the drama I dealt with in school ...

I mean, I have to talk to her about the pictures. And the alcohol. There's no question about that.

I couldn't brush it under the rug and pretend I didn't know.

I had to make sure she was at least using protection if she was considering sex ...

What if she's already had sex? I shuddered at the thought of it.

But what could I do about it if she was?

She's not a child anymore.

I couldn't take her phone away – she needed it for safety.

I looked around the sweet, childlike room. It was in stark contrast to the girl who had that racy photo on her phone.

But love makes you do crazy things.

If anyone could understand that, it was me.

If Michael had asked me to send him nudes back in the day, would I have sent them?

I thought about the tickle of his words on my ear, the feathery kisses and the watery smiles and his rough fingers massaging my breasts ...

Yes, I would have.

Because when you're crazy about someone, you'll do almost anything, consequences be damned.

I opened and closed Delaney's dresser drawers. I sifted through tangles of clothes in her closet.

There was nothing – no pot, no pills, no whips or

chains, no deadly secrets hiding between the sheets or inside the drawers.

Just a picture of a boy, that's all.

I can handle that. After all, there are worse things a teen can do.

I had to talk to her.

Talk, not lecture, I decided. I wanted her to be able to open up to me. I never had that in a mother – a person to confide in – and I craved to be that person for Delaney. The person who made her feel safe, the person she could talk to and trust.

But does anyone trust their parents at this age? I don't know … it's hard to say when I've never experienced it …

I turned her lights back out and tightly wedged her door shut.

Somewhere in the house, I could hear my own cell phone ringing.

I ran for it, digging through my purse, desperately.

"Laney, baby?" I answered, breathily.

"Mom …" She sounded like my little girl again.

"How's Sam? Is she okay?" I closed my eyes, saying another silent prayer despite my ignorance on all things prayer related.

"She's going to be alright, I think. But her neck is broken. It could have been so much worse, Mom. She was *this* close to damaging her windpipe. And of course, if she'd damaged her spine …" I could imagine Laney on the other end, nibbling her lip and the flesh of her inner cheek.

I wish I could be there to soothe her.

"That sounds awful, but, like you said, it could have been so much worse. That must have been so scary for you and your dad."

"And the twins … they're too young to understand, and Dad is going to need my help with them, and a babysitter, until she heals."

The twins.

Something I would never get used to hearing. Unlike me, Samantha had given birth to two happy, healthy twin boys.

"Will she have to have surgery?" I asked, sitting on the edge of my bed. Unlike Delaney's bed, mine was unmade – a twisted tangle of sheets perched in the middle like a blobby white ghost.

"No. But she will have to wear a brace for several weeks and possibly do physical therapy."

"Sounds like a long road ahead. Is there anything I can do for you all? Any way I can help?"

I expected Delaney to snap at me like she'd done earlier, but she simply replied, "Thanks for offering, but I can't think of anything. We're going to stay the night here. They set us up with some cots and a play pen for the boys. Hopefully, she'll get released tomorrow or Sunday."

"Do they know what happened? Who crashed into her?"

Madison was a small town; most of us knew each other or knew *of* each other.

Delaney was quiet on the other end for several seconds.

"You still there, sweetheart?"

"Yeah, sorry. Got distracted. Honestly, I don't know who it was."

"Well, no worries. I was just being nosy. I'm relieved to hear she's okay," I said, and I meant it. I wanted my daughter to be happy, even if that meant she enjoyed spending time with another motherly figure that wasn't me.

"Happy birthday, Mom," Delaney said, catching me off guard. "I'm sorry I didn't tell you earlier. I guess ... I don't know ... I'm just stubborn sometimes. And I should have said it earlier, but then this happened and ... I forgot. I love you and I'm sorry I'm not home to celebrate with you. Remember those cakes we used to make?"

I pinched my eyes shut, fighting back tears.

"Yes, of course I do," I said, unable to hide the shake in my voice. "I miss doing that." Tears tickled the corner of each eye. It felt so good to hear my daughter, my Delaney, again.

"I wish you were here, too, but your dad and Sam and your brothers need you now. We'll have our cakes later."

"Love you," Delaney said again. I thought about the picture on her phone, the inevitable conversation we'd have to have when she got home ...

But for now, I just wanted to enjoy my daughter not hating me.

"I love you too, Laney Bug. I'll talk to you tomorrow."

I clicked end and clutched the phone to my chest. Finally,

I could let the tears spill over, but then my phone buzzed, vibrating against chest.

This time it was Pam.

Don't forget to check out the dating site! I want all the deets when you do!

I groaned. The irritation I'd felt earlier fluttered back, but then instantly dissipated. Maybe it was the high from Delaney's call or the traces of liquor ... but, for the first time, I wondered if joining the site might be fun.

It couldn't hurt, could it?

And I'm sure they had good intentions when they set me up a profile on the site.

Michael had moved on with his new family. And Delaney ... Delaney was getting older and developing love interests of her own.

Apparently.

I have to start dating again some time. Maybe there's no better time than now.

Inside my purse, I found the crumpled piece of paper with the username and password on it.

Should I?

I could imagine Pam beside me saying, *'Hell yes, you silly bitch. Do it!'*

Delaney had swiped the wine, but she didn't know about the stash in my bedroom. I unlocked the tiny metal safe in my closet. Beside the handgun and cash, there were two miniature bottles of whiskey. I grabbed a cold Coke and tumbler from the kitchen, then sat down at the computer with my drink. Nervously, I added the whiskey and logged onto the site.

After a few long swigs, I mustered up enough courage to click "publish" on my new dating profile.

What's the worst that could happen?

Chapter 5

NOW

What's the worst that could happen?
Well, I'll tell you what. Dead bodies. Two of them. And not a clue what to do with either.

At the kitchen table, I gripped my glass of whiskey, swishing it round and around in my hands. This time, there was no Coke. Just me and the glass and the whiskey.

Although a stiff drink was highly needed now, it wasn't a good idea – I had several tasks to complete, and one involved driving.

The dead man's car was still parked outside. I couldn't see it from the kitchen in the dark, but I could feel it there – a warning pulse, sending shivers up and down my spine.

I must get rid of that car.

For once, I was glad that Delaney was staying the night with Michael.

Which means I have all night to fix things.

I still hadn't located the man's ID, but I'd found the keys to his sleek ride tucked inside the visor. The registration and insurance in the glove box identified him as Robin Regal, a name that meant absolutely nothing to me.

But there was an address—and that itself was slightly familiar. Robin Regal lived on Grant Street, in what I guessed was an apartment in the business district of Madison.

I know his name now, but who is he exactly?

I'd never been to his house, but I knew the area.

How did he get here, and why did he come?

I'd gone on several dates over the last few weeks, but not with this man, and not with anyone from my own town of Madison.

He wasn't a friend of Michael's, not someone I knew from work.

There was nothing to connect us.

Nothing except for the fact that his body's here and his car is sitting out front.

If it was just him, maybe I would have called the cops, but the other body. That was the one that really troubled me.

That is the one I'm responsible for, I know it.

I peeked through the side of the blinds. My neighbor Fran usually went to bed around nine or ten which meant I had about an hour to make plans.

It had been years since I'd gone down to the grimy old

cellar underneath our house. But slowly, I descended the steps, the slaps of my bare feet echoing grimly in the hollow space. Using the flashlight app on my phone, I shone it around in the dark. The dank space smelled earthy and was filthier than I remembered. Cobwebs clung to the corners, glistening eerily in the dark, and my heart skipped a beat as a cockroach scuttled across my bare foot.

I held the phone out, looking for more creepy crawlies. I had no doubt they were there, those beady eyes and fat, bulging bodies hiding in the rafters, watching me from the musty black corners of the room …

My light hovered over three black shapes in the corner.

Three long bags were propped against the wall – Michael's old golf bags. There was a time when he just *had* to have them, but just like his interest in me, his obsession with golfing waned, then fizzled out completely. Now I was stuck with his clubs, taking up space, collecting dust in every crevice of my life …

One by one, I laid the clunky, black bags on their sides, and started unloading the clubs. They clanked on the concrete floor, hopefully scaring away any nearby critters.

When all three bags were empty, I tugged them up the stairs, one by one. Even empty, the thick, glossy leather was heavy. Back in my room, I laid the bags on the floor beside the bodies.

What seemed like a good idea at first now seemed silly. Each bag was over five feet, Robin Regal was nearly six.

This isn't going to work.

Nice plan, Ivy.

My face paled, my stomach twisting in knots, as the realization kicked in: if I wanted to fit the bodies into the bags, I'd have to cut them into pieces to do it.

Chapter 6

BEFORE

His name was Richard. Six foot four, two hundred pounds – I felt like a tiny bird standing next to him at my height of five foot five.

I won't lie – I was fully expecting him to look older, heavier, and less attractive than the photos on his dating profile. But Richard was surprisingly better-looking than I could have imagined. The conversation was a little dense; he mostly talked about boats and motor-cross sports as he poked at the mozzarella-cheese-stick appetizer he had insisted I "had to try".

"That sounds like a lot of work," I remarked, between bites, listening to him describe the tedious process of rebuilding the motor in his Yamaha Raptor 660.

Truth be told, I didn't know anything about four-wheelers, and I didn't really care to either. But it was refreshing – eating dinner with a nice, handsome man and discussing something other than robo-calls with Pam and Jerry at work or arguing with Delaney or Michael at home.

As he described his plans for adding new pistons and rings, I tried to imagine what he looked like naked. He was in shape, chest muscles flexing under his soft grey t-shirt. And below the table he was wearing a perfect-fitting pair of stonewashed jeans.

How long has it been since I had sex?

And I'd never had it with a random guy, someone I wasn't dating.

His eyes were chocolate brown, his lashes long for a man. I rested my chin in my hands, listening, all the while thinking about those eyes and how they would look peering down into mine while he fucked me ...

"You guys know what ya want for dinner?" Our perky blonde waitress was back, ponytail swishing back and forth as she rocked impatiently on the balls of her feet.

My cell phone rang in my purse. "You go ahead and order first," I told Richard.

I pushed my chair back and stood up. "Hi, sweetheart."

I held up one finger to Richard and the waitress and walked off from the table so I could hear Delaney.

"Mom! Are you busy?" Delaney's voice sounded breathy and strange.

I glanced back at my date; he was laughing, the waitress leaning over, exposing her cleavage. She was young and gorgeous, way younger and prettier than me at my forty years. Richard seemed to agree with my assessment ...

"No, I'm not. What's going on? Is Samantha okay?"

Delaney groaned. "Well, that's the thing. She's alright but she's still having a lot of pain. Dad took her to the doctor this morning. I thought they'd be back by now, but I can't get hold of them. Dad's not picking up."

I flexed my jaw. "Is there something wrong?" Michael had probably left his phone in the car while he went inside, knowing him.

"It's Braxton."

One of the twins.

It was strange hearing her say her brother's name; she rarely mentioned the boys to me.

"Is he okay?" I asked, tentatively. Delaney was the designated babysitter again, apparently. She had been helping Samantha a lot this week, and although that shouldn't have annoyed me, it kind of did. Delaney was a teenager, and capable of babysitting ... but two young twins was a lot of work for anyone, especially a young, teenage girl with a growing amount of homework each night.

"I'm not sure. He felt hot, so I looked everywhere and finally found a thermometer. His temperature is 102. Is that high? According to Web MD, it is ..."

"Yes, that's pretty high," I said, glancing down at my watch. I was nearly an hour away from Madison. "Is he fussy?"

"Well, he was for a while ... but now he seems lethargic and sweaty. I'm scared, Mom. Can you come?"

"Of course. I'm about an hour away, but I'll try to get there as fast as I can. In the meantime, if he's wearing any clothes, take them off. Just leave his diaper on him for now. And make sure he's drinking; we don't want him to get dehydrated."

"Okay. Please hurry. But drive carefully," Delaney said, shakily. I could tell she was frightened and unsure.

"See you soon. Love you."

I ended the call and jogged back to the table.

"I'm so sorry—" For a moment, I couldn't remember my date's name.

"Richard," I rebounded, "my daughter needs me. Could we do this another time?"

Richard took a sip of his beer and set it down with a thud. "I thought you only had one grown child."

"She's not grown. She's a teenager. And she needs me. Thanks for the appetizer," I said, slightly annoyed by his less-than-thoughtful reaction.

I turned to leave.

"So, I guess I'll be paying for this myself, huh?" I felt my entire body recoil.

"Here." I opened my purse, dug around for my wallet. Finally, I took out two tens and a five. I dropped them in the center of the plate with the greasy, disgusting cheese sticks.

***

I'd been to Michael and Samantha's home hundreds of time. But never inside it.

Today, instead of parking at the curb and refusing to look at the place like I usually did, I whipped my minivan into the driveway. It was wide enough for four cars; no reason I couldn't park here – it's just that usually, I didn't want to.

I placed the van in park and stepped out, my eyes straying warily over the two-story miniature mansion that Michael called his home now. On the outside, the house looked old and stood out like a lovely thumb among its more modern neighbors. The paint on the siding was rustic and off-white, but it looked purposefully charming. There were window boxes full of sunflowers and daisies, a cute little red-hatted gnome by the steps leading up to the covered porch. I strode toward it, admiring the smooth, polished stones that lined that concrete pathway to the house.

The screen door was laced with little flowers and curls. I opened it and stepped inside.

I'd never been this far, always dropping Delaney at the curb, or a few times, walking her up to the screen. I don't know what I was expecting – I guess something sleeker and more modern once I entered, especially after all the renovations they'd supposedly been doing.

But the front porch was lined with old-fashioned, knotty pine rockers, and several hanging plants that appeared to be carefully cared for. I knocked on a thick green door.

I tried to be patient, adjusting my heavy black purse in the crook of my arm, and glancing around wearily.

If Michael and Samantha pull in, this will be quite awkward.

I couldn't see a doorbell anywhere. I knocked harder with the side of my fist, then finally, I tried the knob. It was unlocked.

"Laney?" I cracked the door open an inch and shouted her name.

After what felt like several minutes, I pushed the door all the way in and peeked inside.

There was a corridor, long and tight, and I walked tentatively down bright red carpet until it opened into a fancy entryway. A glass table set in the center of the room; a massive vase of daisies displayed as the center-piece beneath a glittering chandelier that must have cost thousands.

"Laney?" I shouted again. I relieved myself of my purse, plopping the old bag on the table next to the flowers. There was a steep, wooden staircase leading to the second floor, but first I peeked into the maze of doorways that led off the entry. An enormous kitchen, with black and white tiles and new, stainless-steel appliances that looked neat, but rather complicated. A bathroom, with a fancy pedestal sink and commode. A cozy living room, with two leather loveseats and the biggest oak coffee-table I'd ever seen, situated in front of an ornate fireplace.

There was no one around.

As I ascended the stairs, right hand gripping the sleek wooden bannister, I called out for my daughter again.

This time, my words bounced back at me, echoing up the twisty stairs.

The second-floor hallway was carpeted with the same ugly red carpet as downstairs. I quickly found a switch in the hallway, and dull yellow light revealed a hallway papered in blue-black stripes and lined with neatly framed family photos.

Michael and Samantha's wedding photos. Samantha, in tight overalls with her hair in a bandanna, gripping a thick paintbrush layered with sunny yellow paint.

Where are all the pictures of Delaney? I wondered, a flicker of irritation rolling through me. *And where the hell is my daughter?*

It wasn't unusual for Delaney to ignore me at home, but she'd called me for help.

If Braxton is sick, why don't I hear him?

The first door on the right was closed. I tried to ease it open, but it creaked, giving my heart a small jumpstart.

I let out a low whistle as I saw what lay inside. Hardback books, lined from floor to ceiling, on one wall. Another low set of shelves lined with dusty encyclopedias. And the far-left wall was left open ... there was an enormous mural painted there, but it didn't look finished. Three unicorns with wings, flying through a maze of clouds. On the back of one of them, was a girl. Dark hair, moon-shaped eyes, but only half of her body was finished.

She looks just like Delaney. Monstrously beautiful.

"Mom." I lurched at the sound of Delaney whisper-shouting behind me.

"Jesus! You scared me." I held a hand to my chest. "I knocked and knocked, and I've been calling for you ..."

Delaney pressed one finger to her lips. She whispered, "Sorry. This house is so big. Sound doesn't always travel well."

Was that a slight at me? A nasty reminder that our house was small, compared to this magnificent beast of a house that her father gave her?

But Delaney's face showed no signs of malice. Her eyes were puffy with sleep, her cheeks red.

"Are you okay?" I asked, remembering at the last second to keep my voice low.

"Yeah," Delaney yawned. "I just got him down for a nap. To be honest, I fell asleep with him for a bit. What took you so long to get here?" Her eyes narrowed slightly; she had become my *new daughter* again.

"I was in Butchertown, doing a little shopping," I lied. "Where's Braxton? Can I see him?"

"This way."

I followed Delaney to the end of the hall, eyes averting more happy photos on the wall. She pressed her finger to her lips a second time, then motioned me inside one of the bedrooms.

This was her room, obviously. Nine Inch Nails and Nirvana posters lined the walls. An old soul with great taste, I had to admit. She had shiny black furniture, a modern dresser and wardrobe. A cool black checkered chair in the corner.

In the center of the bed, a little blonde angel was sleeping. I approached the boy, cautiously holding my breath.

I'd seen the twins several times, mostly while stalking photos on Samantha's Facebook page. But there was something different about seeing him in person, and so close up.

For the first time, I realized how much he looked like Delaney. Sure, he was blonde, and she was dark, but with his eyes closed in sleep, he could have been her at age two. His lashes were long, cheeks dimpled. Like a monstrous little cherub.

I pressed my hand on his forehead. He was hot, his rosy-red cheeks and ragged breathing an instant giveaway that he was sick. Maybe some sort of virus ...

When I glanced back at Delaney, I was surprised to see her still standing by the door. Arms crossed over her chest, she looked uncomfortable ... *guilty*.

She feels bad about asking me to come. She's worried it upsets me, seeing her half-brother, being in this house ...

"Good job at getting him down for a nap. He does still seem to have a mild fever, but I definitely think it's less than 102."

Delaney gave me a tired smile. "I gave him some children's Tylenol I found and took his clothes off and cooled him down with a wet rag." She stuck her chin out and stood straighter – I could tell she felt proud of herself.

"Great job, honey. You are such a good big sister."

"Thanks," she said, awkwardly, shifting foot to foot.

"Where's the other boy?" I asked.

Delaney rolled her eyes. "The other boy's name is Brock. He's asleep across the hall. I thought I should probably keep them as separate as possible, so he doesn't catch whatever this is too ..."

"Smart thinking." Instinctually, I reached out to tuck her hair behind her ear. She flinched slightly but let me do it. "What about you? How are you feeling?"

She, too, was looking red and blistery. I held the back of my hand to her forehead.

"Mom! I'm fine!" she shouted.

Braxton stirred and made a small moan; we both froze and looked over at him.

He itched his tiny nose with his right hand, but his eyes never opened.

"I should go check on Brock," Delaney whispered.

"No, let me. If you're sick, you could pass it to him. Although, there's a good chance he'll get it anyway if it's viral ..."

Across the hall, I nudged the door. It opened into another bright white room. Two toddler beds in the center, a neat array of toy bins and shelves with books lining each side of the room. It was like looking into a mirror, each side matching the other.

A perfect room for twins.

My heart splintered and cracked as I sat down on the empty bed, looking at Braxton's other half. Brock was asleep, snoring softly. Although the boys were identical, Brock's blonde locks were slightly longer, curls tickling the tops of his ears and hanging low in his eyes. There was a soft, velvety frog on the bed beside him.

Dillan.

The two D's and the two B's …

I often wondered if Michael and I would still be together if we hadn't lost a son. His death changed me, in the way that death often does, and we grew up.

More than that – we grew to hate each other, I guess.

"You lost your parents. You should be able to handle this," Michael had told me once.

I hated him for that comment. As much as it hurt losing Mom and Dad, losing children is something else entirely.

The fact was that I was too busy mourning my son and raising my daughter to notice that my marriage was unraveling. I'd had no idea he was having an affair. Looking back now, all the signs were there – the late nights at work, the last-minute travel, the closely guarded cell phone …

I stared at the boy, his gentle snores like soft like kitten purrs. I tried to imagine him with darker hair, slightly darker skin.

Is this what Dillan would have looked like?

"Dad just sent me a message." Dazed, I looked up to find Delaney watching me from the doorway. She was leaning against the frame, her eyes soft and filled with sadness. "They're on their way back."

I stood up and adjusted the blankets around the boy,

showing Delaney that I wasn't heartless – that I knew this boy was her brother and that I cared for him too because of that ...

"Did your father say why he didn't answer your calls?"

"He was so worried about Sam that he rushed her in and left his cell phone behind in the car."

Just as I suspected. Worried about his wife ... but what about Delaney? What about his other children?

"Did you tell him about Braxton?" I asked, unclenching my teeth. Michael had always been selfish, and he compartmentalized everything. If one thing goes wrong, he can't deal with the rest ...

Sure, Delaney was old enough to help with her siblings, but still ...

He shouldn't put everything on her while Samantha is healing, and he should most certainly keep his phone nearby in case of emergencies.

"Yeah. They're going to be here any minute."

That mask of discomfort was back. Delaney didn't want them to return home and find me – *the evil ex* – in their lovely paradise house.

"Okay. Well, I'll leave you to it then." I gave her a light kiss on the cheek and once again, she recoiled. "Why don't you come home tonight? You're looking a little peaked yourself. I could fix you some soup, take care of you for a change ... I'm sure your dad can handle the twins." But I wasn't sure about that at all, to be honest.

"Nah. I'll be fine. I'll take some Tylenol and have a nap

when they get here." Delaney turned and started walking down the long, dark hallway, leading me out of the house.

"I'd really like you home soon. There are things I'd like to discuss with you, and catching up to do. Plus, I'm sure you're behind on your homework."

"I'm not behind," Delaney snapped. "What *things* do you want to talk about?" She chewed her lip, looking worried.

My mind drifted back to that photo.

Who was the boy that sent it?

"I just want to catch up with you, Laney. Get some rest. I need to get going."

Delaney said no more, just watched anxiously from the top of the staircase, as I saw myself back downstairs.

In the grand entryway, I gathered up my purse and took one last sweeping gaze around the room. There was another door downstairs I hadn't entered, and with one glance, I knew it was Michael and Samantha's room.

The bed was partially unmade, a heap of men's clothing piled haphazardly on the floor. The small mess looked out of place with the glitzy mirrored walls and the chic pink vanity in the corner. Neat bottles of perfume and gold packs of makeup lined Samantha's space. In the mirror, I could see her face, smiling sweetly at herself as she powdered her nose and cheeks. And looking past her own reflection in the mirror, her eyes meeting Michael's, as he watched her getting ready ...

Michael always did like women who "took care of themselves", as he put it. I was never the type – I bought cheap mascara from CVS and rarely wore jewelry or perfume.

Maybe it wasn't the loss of Dillan. Maybe our relationship had been doomed from the start.

I wasn't his type. And let's face it, he wasn't mine either.

Suddenly, I heard the thud of a car door slamming out front.

With a jolt, I darted across the hall, then slipped inside the kitchen. Through the curtains above the sink, I saw Michael walk around the front of his truck. Samantha was in the passenger seat; I could see she was wearing a neck brace still.

He gave my van an irritated look as he wrenched open Samantha's passenger door and began helping her out of the truck.

"Shit."

I started looking around for another exit. It was stupid; they knew I was here. There was no getting around that, but I didn't want to come face to face with them, didn't want to have to explain why I was here.

There was a mudroom connected to the kitchen. I scooted past a stackable washer and dryer and a messy shoe stand in the corner. Finally, I let myself out the side door beside the shoe stand, hoping I'd come out on the side of the house. And hopefully, by the time I made it around to the van, Michael and Samantha would already be inside.

I heard the jangle of keys in the front door lock, and with an itchy sense of panic, I closed the door behind me.

Dull sunlight coated my face, a welcoming relief. The door did in fact lead to the side of the house.

This part of the yard was hidden from view from the front by thick shrubbery. It offered a decidedly less pleasant view. Thick green algae licked up the sides of the weathered old house.

As I made my way around front, I passed a rickety, out-of-place carport. Samantha's Beemer was parked beneath it. There was a deep gash in the side of it, ugly and long.

Why haven't they had this fixed yet? I wondered. *God knows they can afford to.*

Grateful to find Michael and Samantha gone as I curled around the side of the house, I climbed behind the wheel of my van and backed out, shuddering at the monstrous old house my daughter considered home.

Chapter 7

BEFORE

"Don't move again," Pam breathed. Her breath, minty and hot, blew in my face as she sighed. She licked the pad of her thumb and rubbed something off the corner of my eye lid.

Jerry was stretched out on my bed, eyes closed, flipping through an outdated National Geographic with the headline, '*WAS DARWIN WRONG?*'

"It was just annoying, that's all. The house was perfect ... so eerily unblemished ..." I said, telling them about my tour of Casa de Michael.

"Unlike your face if you don't stop talking." Pam stepped back, eyes searching crazily, then announced, "You look perfect. I'd fuck you."

"You're nasty," Jerry said, throwing the magazine at her.

"Yes, she is." I whipped around to look in the mirror.

I didn't look perfect, but I *did* look good. My makeup was flawless despite Pam's teasing, and my hair was bone-straight and shiny thanks to Pam's ultra-expensive straightening iron.

I'd bought a new shirt for the occasion, too, a soft grey V-neck with tiny sequins. It matched my black leggings and combat boots.

"I still think you look too ... I don't know ... dark?" Pam pondered. She was jamming her makeup brushes into a gold, plastic pouch, then she stopped to give my mostly black outfit a full look-over.

"I want to look like myself," I sighed. "Remember that corny quote about 'like me for me'? Well, I believe that shit. As naïve as it may sound ..."

"You're right. But do you have to wear those shoes? You look like you're going to stomp a hole in someone's ass," Jerry teased.

"These aren't shoes. They're boots. And they're my favorite, if you really must know." I walked over to the full-length mirror, ducking down a couple inches to see my whole face.

"Fuck it. I'm ready."

***

Pam and Jerry saw me off, like two proud yet overly critical parents. A few hours later, I was sitting in a diner with Boston456, otherwise known as a Ben Blankenbaker.

Unlike Richard, who had impressed me with his looks and repelled me with his behavior, Ben was quite the opposite.

Admittedly, I was a little disappointed when I saw him hunched under the awning at Cineplex 4. He looked five or six years older than his profile picture on the dating site and at least fifty pounds heavier.

But who was I to judge? My pics and bio weren't me either, not exactly. And marking my age as thirty was plumb ridiculous.

My profile was a reflection of who I wanted to be ... a mere ghost of who I really was.

But I had to admit, Ben had a great smile. And his eyes were soft and smiley too – the sort of eyes you might call "kind". His whole face lit up when he saw me. He was also unlike Richard in that he seemed genuinely interested in what I had to say. He asked questions about Delaney, instantly making me feel at ease.

I was the one who suggested going to see a movie. After the catastrophe with Richard, it seemed like a good idea. But once we were seated in the middle aisle, crammed between a rowdy group of teens and a few middle-aged couples, I couldn't help wishing for the solitude and intimacy of a quiet restaurant.

Ben let me pick the movie, which was nice of him, but I'm not a big movie or TV person. I'd pored over my choices the night before: horror was too iffy – some people hate scary flicks, although I like them from time to time – and romance had seemed like an awkward choice, considering we didn't know each other.

"You should pick that new DC movie. Or Marvel, whatever the hell is," Jerry had suggested. "Men love those movies."

No way.

As much as I wanted to pick a movie we'd both like, action movies weren't my thing.

Finally, I'd settled on a drama.

"I haven't seen the previews for this, but I like Jake Gyllenhaal," Ben whispered to me in the dark. "I'm just glad you didn't pick a superhero movie. I know people love them but they're not my thing."

"Oh, thank God. Mine neither," I said, through a mouthful of buttery popcorn.

Ben had splurged on the snacks – an extra-large bucket of popcorn, several boxes of candy, and two mountainous blue Icees.

"I know I'm heavier in real life than in my pictures. Sorry about that. I just love eating, you know?" As he said it, I giggled at his stained blue teeth.

"Same here. I'd rather eat what I want than worry about my weight," I admitted.

An older gentleman in the row behind us let out a spit-riddled 'shhh'. Ben and I gave each other startled looks, then snorted with laughter.

We made it through an hour of the movie. The acting was great, but the drama was slow ... and depressing.

When Ben leaned over and suggested we grab coffee to wake ourselves up, I was relieved.

I wanted to talk to him more.

And that was how we got here – sitting knee to knee across from each other, drinking pumpkin spice lattes and laughing.

I liked him. *Really* liked him, not in that forcing-myself-to-try kind of way that I had with Richard at first. Ben seemed funny and genuine, and the more he talked, the more attractive he became.

Like me, he worked in sales. Only, his focus was on computers, whereas we sold a mixture of things at Bradley and Benson Inc.

We exchanged our funniest customer service stories and vented about pay. And I talked about Delaney – which I hadn't planned on doing. But when he opened up about his own son and showed me pictures, I had felt comfortable showing mine. He was divorced like me and had only joined Plenty of Fish because his friends and family had pressured him to do so. His son, Joshua, was a couple years younger than Delaney.

"I must admit. This is the best date I've ever had," he said shyly, after pulling out two fives for the tip jar up front. The coffee shop was closing, the patient barista behind the counter breaking down machines and wiping off counters.

"Me too. This was fun," I said, honestly. It *was* fun. And I found myself wondering what our second date would be like.

Truth be told, I wasn't ready for the evening to end. Delaney was still at her father's.

Would it be so bad to invite Ben over for a nightcap?

We had just stepped outside, the heady smell of coffee fading as I was hit with a blast of warm, fall air.

"I'm not quite ready to say good night, but I guess I have to," Ben said, tucking his hands in his jeans awkwardly.

"My daughter's staying with her father tonight. Would you like to come over and have a drink? My house is less than a half hour away ..." I could hear the words flowing out of my mouth, but it sounded like someone else was saying them. Someone confident. Someone unlike me. Someone more like the girl in the profile picture, unfiltered and secure ...

Ben smiled, a thin blue film still staining his lips. "I'd love that," he told me.

Chapter 8

Now

The keys to Robin's apartment were in my palm. I curled my fingers around them, a tingle of fear – or was it anticipation? – rustling through my veins. I'd followed the directions on my phone and just as I had suspected, his address was smack dab in the middle of Madison's historic business district.

The blue Camaro had been fast, the gas pedal touchy, making for a jumpy ride through town. I'd left the windows up and driven the speed limit all the way there.

What if I get pulled over? What would I say? And what if someone sees me?

The questions were like knives, chiseling endless tunnels through my worried brain ...

But I'd made it, only passing two or three cars on the way in, the cover of night my welcome companion.

And now I stood in front of the dead man's home, his keys, sweaty with perspiration, gripped tight – too tight – and cutting into my palms.

A shudder of fear rolled through me.

The building was pitch black, not a single light shining from above. It was a narrow building, squeezed between a used bookstore and an old-fashioned Italian diner that also looked closed and somewhat abandoned. It was eleven o'clock, an oppressive hush falling over every single storefront on the block.

I'd parked the Camaro at the curb, pleasantly surprised to find only a few cars nearby. Most of these old buildings were used for what they were made for – small businesses. But not for Mr. Regal. My guess was that he was renting the top half of 408 Grant Street.

I pressed my nose to the grimy glass storefront on the bottom level. There was an ornate oak bar to the right, a cluster of six tiny tables to the left. There were no bottles of alcohol behind the bar, and from what I could see, the tables looked sticky with a layer of dust.

Like many businesses in Madison, this one must have flopped too.

I stepped back from the window and looked up. There were two windows on the second story, both thickly shaded with blinds.

The door to the restaurant was locked. I was sure of that, and I didn't dare try to tug on the door, for fear of setting off some sort of alarm. My guess was that the residential entrance was in the back.

Keeping my head down, tucked low to my chest, I followed the uneven sidewalk around the block where I discovered a skinny alley. My footsteps echoed in the dark as I approached the back of the mystery man's building, still clutching the keys in a vise-like grip.

The backside was dumpy, a shiny metal dumpster overflowing with garbage beside a thick red door with chipped paint.

My hands shook as I started trying keys in the lock. I couldn't shake the feeling that I was being watched, even though I couldn't see or hear anyone.

If anything, I'll probably see a racoon out here, rustling around in that putrid garbage.

There were four keys on Robin Regal's key chain. The key to his Camaro, a tiny silver key that looked like it went to a locker or gun safe, and two shiny gold keys that resembled house keys.

The first gold key fit easily into the lock. When it turned, I should have felt relief, but instead I felt more afraid. What – or who – was inside? And what if someone saw me breaking into this building?

The first thing I noticed when I stepped inside, besides the inky blackness, was how cramped the entryway was. My shin banged against something in the dark as I struggled to find enough room to close the front door behind me.

I popped on my flashlight app with a swipe of my thumb.

My eyes traveled up, up, up ... There were two steep flights of stairs leading straight up into the darkness. Beside the staircase was a narrow walkway that seemed to lead to the unused bar I'd seen from the front side.

I bent down and rubbed my shin, realizing it had struck the first sturdy wooden step.

There was nowhere to go but up, the tiny stamp of floor in the entryway barely big enough for one person, let alone two.

I gripped the wobbly bannister and started climbing, my trepidation replaced with something else I hadn't felt in a long time: curiosity.

The top of the first set of steps revealed a similarly tight square of wood, but there were two white doors on either side of the landing. I knocked softly on the left-hand door, surprised when it wobbled a few inches forward. Taking a deep breath of courage, I nudged it the rest of the way open with my foot.

As my eyes slowly adjusted to the darkness, a room full of blobby white ghosts came into view. Without stepping inside, I stuck one hand in and felt around for a switch. There was a tiny popping sound, and then the room flooded with sick yellow light.

The blobby white ghosts were sheets, and they appeared to be covering up unused furniture. Nervously, I stepped inside the room. I didn't have to lift the sheets to know what was under them – tables and chairs scattered around the massive room.

It was huge, like a studio apartment, but not the fancy kind you imagine you'll find in places like New York. The wooden plank flooring was scarred with age, the bumpy painted walls streaked with mildew and mold.

I turned the light off and wedged the door back shut.

Maybe he doesn't really live here. Or ... he could be the owner of the restaurant, who knows?

The room across the hall was also unlocked. It, too, was used for storage. Mostly cooking supplies and a large greasy deep fryer set in the corner.

Finally, I ascended the next set of stairs. Expecting another landing with empty apartments, I was shocked to find myself stepping straight into a large open space. I held my light out in front of me at the top of the staircase, looking around in awe. The entire top floor was a huge apartment with exposed brick and ductwork.

Finally, there's room to move around.

But then I remembered ... I don't belong here, and how do I know no one's home?

"Hello?" My voice sounded like someone else's, a meek little mouse.

Unlike the crowded rooms used for storage downstairs, this one had only a few modest furnishings. Cracked leather sofa in the center of the room. Coffee table stacked with books.

There were no doors separating the rooms, one section flowing straight into the next like a wide-mouthed stream. I tiptoed through the sitting area and entered a large bedroom space. A tall bed with a gold frame faced two windows. I crept over to one of them and pulled up the blinds. From here, I could see the street in front of the restaurant, the dead man's Camaro still parked at the curb.

"Who the hell are you?" I asked, turning my back to the windows and staring at the neatly made bed. There was a nightstand, two chunky wood dressers, and a pair of scruffy house shoes lined up perfectly.

Tentatively, I started opening and closing drawers. As expected, the clothes inside were neatly folded, white t-shirts rolled into perfect rows. Even his underwear – also plain white – was folded.

I left the bedroom, strolling back to the sitting area. The books were standard classics – not surprising, I guess. I looked around the beautiful, chic brick walls. No pictures whatsoever and only one painting.

And what it depicted sent chills down my spine.

There were two women in it – well, at first, I thought they were women – heads and necks like human women, but with the torsos and talons of a bird. The bird-woman on the right looked happy and bright, but the other ... her hair and wings were dark, her eyes ringed with blackness, her mouth opened as though she were moaning in pain.

I couldn't imagine why anyone would want this on their wall.

But then again, there was something intriguing about it – the light and the dark, the happiness and the sorrow. The two sides of ourselves we can never escape.

I had to pull my face away from it as I advanced towards the kitchen. But those bird-women ... I could feel their eyes burrowing into the back of my head as I scanned the kitchen counter and sifted through several neat, organized drawers.

Nothing. Not a damn thing to tell me who he is, or why the hell he was in my apartment.

In a small alcove off the kitchen, I located the bathroom. It was the first and only room that seemed to have a door of its own.

It was in here that I found my first clue.

Like the rest of the apartment, the bathroom was neat and pristine. But the bundle of pill bottles under the sink told a different story. Robin Regal was a sick man. He was taking medicine to treat cancer and a laundry list of pain and anxiety medications ...

But the name on the bottle didn't say Robin Regal.

With trembling fingers, I held one of them up closer to the dim lightbulb over the sink.

I knew this name. And it was one I hadn't heard in a very long time.

Chapter 9

1993 – Andrea

*P*hilomena Nordstrom.

Even her name made me think of money.

The new girl – well, if you consider joining Riverbank Junior High two years ago *new*.

In a school of fewer than 600 students, Philomena was destined to be the only "new girl" for years to come.

And it didn't hurt that she was also pretty ... and rich. A new cable company had moved to our small town of Lafayette, and with it came the Nordstrom family. Philomena's father owned the company; Philomena, the lovely, black-haired beauty, was his only daughter. Her mother was a stay-at-home mom who looked barely ten years older than her knockout of a daughter.

I was her polar opposite: hair the color of dirty dishwater, skin bumpy like oatmeal, family unknown. Poor as dirt.

I'd heard people talk about "old souls". I'd like to think I have one of those ... In reality, I was older than my four-teen years because I'd lost my parents at age ten and been raised by my less-than-kind uncle ever since. His job at the toothpaste factory paid very little, and most nights I struggled to find something in the cupboards to feed myself.

He was gone a lot, either working or drinking – and I saw that as a bonus most of the time. But the dank one-bedroom trailer we lived in – me on the couch, him in the room – was lonely sometimes.

But it's not lonely today.

Philomena Nordstrom was here. I liked that part, but what I didn't like were the others: Mandy Billingsworth and Tamara Thompson, Philomena's closest sidekicks. They weren't sold on the idea of partying in my uncle's dumpy trailer, but Philomena didn't seem to mind it.

"Do you like this color, Andrea?" We were seated on my bed, knees touching, my hand face down on her upper thigh. Her legs were tan and glossy, and up close, she was even prettier, to be honest.

"Yes, it's perfect."

Tamara and Mandy giggled from where they sat on the carpet. Probably laughing at me, but I didn't care. I refused to even look over at them, eyes trained on the slick coats of polish, dark purple like a fresh, pretty bruise.

They were drinking and smoking pot. I knew that sooner or later I'd have to join them or else risk looking like the loser I really was. But Philomena wasn't drinking either, I'd noticed. She held my hand gently on her thigh, gliding the brush over my nails, using practiced strokes like a trained artist.

"You two are cute together," Tamara grunted with laughter, then stuck her tongue out and wiggled it at us both.

"Ignore them. They're small-brained," Philomena said, gently rolling my pinky so she could get the hard-to-reach edges with her brush.

I looked up at her, and for a moment we locked gazes. Her smile was wide and full of mischief.

"What time is it? I want mine done next," Mandy whined from the carpet.

"It's almost ten o'clock," I said, a thick knot forming in the back of my throat. I stole another glance at Philomena, but she was concentrating intensely on my left thumbnail.

If she only knew that when midnight arrived, her friends were going to kill her.

Chapter 10

BEFORE

It felt good having Delaney back under my roof. She was still under the weather a bit, but that wasn't the reason she was locked inside her room.

The only reason she was here tonight was because I'd called and hassled Michael until he agreed. She was sick, and probably behind on her schoolwork. She needed a break from playing babysitter/caretaker to Samantha and her brothers.

When Delaney was angry, she was a hard cookie to crack ... but one thing I knew she couldn't resist: cheap Chinese takeout from Double Dragon.

As I laid out paper plates and opened steaming cartons of food, I could already hear her shuffling around in her room.

"Oh, hey Pam." I held my phone to my ear. "Can I

call you back? Just had Double Dragon delivered and I'm starving ..."

I hung up from my fake phone call – a pathetic maneuver if I'm being honest with myself – and pulled out a chair. I was scooping chicken fried rice and crab rangoons on a clean white plate when the door to Delaney's room swung open.

Despite her sour mood earlier, she was wearing a reluctant smile. She took a seat at the table across from me, then began filling her own plate with food.

"You totally faked that phone call, didn't you?" She raised an eyebrow at me.

I choked on a slippery chunk of sesame chicken as I bubbled over with laughter.

"Guilty as charged. I didn't want to eat alone again at the table tonight, and I knew you'd be hungry." Little did Delaney know, I hadn't been eating at the table; instead, I'd been eating where I slept, watching corny shows on Hulu while eating overcooked Lean Cuisines.

It wasn't only because I was missing Delaney; I'd been waiting on Ben to call too. It had been three nights since our first date that turned into an overnight affair and I was disappointed – shocked, really – that he hadn't called or texted. He hadn't even responded to my messages on the dating site where we originally met.

I was embarrassed when Pam asked me how it was going. I'd told her about the date, about the entire night ...

"It's called ghosting. Don't take it personally," she had explained.

But how could I not take it personally?

The date had gone so well – perfectly, in fact. And the sex … the sex had been incredible.

At least for me … What if it hadn't been for him?

"How was school today?" I asked Delaney, forcing myself to shut out thoughts of Ben.

"Fine."

"What did you learn? Anything interesting?"

Delaney's mouth was full of chow mein as she shook her head in annoyance.

I took a few more bites of my food, trying to enjoy the temporary peace at the table. It was about to be blown to bits – possibly – but I had to ask Delaney while I had her here, and had her attention …

"I'm glad we have a chance to talk."

Delaney groaned before I could say another word. I clenched my jaw, a flash of pure rage jolting through me, then evaporating as quickly as it had come.

"The other day when I dropped you off at the hospital and you accidentally dropped your phone …"

Delaney stopped chewing, her eyes zeroing in on mine, daring me to say it …

"I wasn't snooping. But a text message came in … a naked picture."

Delaney took a drink of her Kool-Aid, slurping noisily as I went on, "You're only fifteen, Laney. You can't receive nude photos or send ones of yourself. You're too young for

102

all that, and I'm worried about your safety. Can you tell me who this boy is at least?"

"Nope. I can't." Delaney pushed her chair back and stood up so quickly that for a brief moment, I thought she might reach over and hit me.

"You're fucking unbelievable, you know that?" Her hand swung out and I flinched as she batted a carton of food off the table. Egg rolls hit the floor and spread out like a fan. I stared at the food in silence before raising my eyes to meet Delaney's.

Her own eyes were wide, face shiny pink with fury, and she mashed her hands down angrily on her hips.

My daughter thinks she's a badass. Well, I'm about to show her.

As I leapt to my feet, it was her turn to be scared. In one long sweeping motion I knocked all the food on the floor.

Delaney stared at the food and back at me, a look on her face I hadn't seen in a long time ... *fear.*

We stood there glaring at each other, a standoff that couldn't end well.

"I'm calling Dad," Delaney said with a huff, then turned on her heels and stomped off to her room.

"Good for you. Tell him I said hello," I shouted after her, the fiery rage inside me fizzling out completely. It was replaced with another emotion I knew all too well: unencumbered guilt and pain.

***

That night, I did something I'd never done before. I called Samantha. I would have preferred Michael, but I knew he was working, and I was hoping Samantha might listen to me.

I had her number stored in my phone in case of emergencies, but I never dreamed I'd be using it to discuss parental issues with her.

"She had what on her phone?" Sam asked and I could hear the tiredness in her voice. I imagined her sitting at her lovely vanity table, brushing her long dark hair while she waited for Michael to get off work.

"A naked boy. And I didn't want to confront her about it, but I had to. We had an argument and it got quite heated. I assume she probably called Michael or you, but I don't think we should give in to her demands and let her go back to you and Michael tonight ... not until she talks to me about this boy. I'm just so worried—"

"Ivy," Samantha said, "she hasn't called me or Michael. She only said that to piss you off."

"Oh."

Well, it worked.

I'd never heard Samantha say a cuss word before and frankly, I kind of liked it.

I was standing outside on the back porch, praying Delaney wasn't trying to listen in. The last thing she needed to do was catch me talking about her.

But what does she expect? Michael, Samantha, and I have to be responsible and work together. We're not doing it to be mean; we're doing it because we love her, dammit!

104

"Well, I'm glad she didn't call. She's been locked away in her room since supper, which is fine. If she wants to sulk, then I'll let her sulk for a while. But I'm worried she's sexually active, that maybe we need to discuss birth control options ..."

"She's not," Samantha said, so quiet on the other end.

"Not what?" I said, catching my breath.

"Delaney's not having sex."

"And how can you be so sure of that?" I said, that old familiar flicker of anger returning.

"Because she told me, that's why. Sometimes it's easier for kids to tell their stepmoms these things. I don't know why, but it is."

I tried to steady the shake in my voice before I answered, "Well, I'm glad she talks to you, but she obviously doesn't tell you everything. Unless you also know who the boy in the photo is?"

"I don't know his name, no. But I do know that she's taking an art class at Piedmont."

"What?" I cut in.

"Michael and I are paying for it. She really wanted to go ..."

My mind flashed back to those whimsical paintings in the library.

Why hadn't Delaney shared this interest with me?

As though she could read my mind, Samantha said, "I don't think she wanted to tell anyone yet because she wasn't sure if she'd like it. She's never taken a class like this before, and most of the other students in it are adults. She's incredibly talented though, and I think she needs to harness that gift. You should see these paintings ..."

"I saw them the other day when I was at your house," I said, softly.

"Oh. Sorry, yeah, I forgot about that. Listen, I don't know who the boy is, but I'm guessing it has something to do with an art project she's working on. I don't think it's anything sexual, honestly."

"I guess it's possible ..."

"A boy sending her photos wouldn't interest her much anyway," Samantha said, stiffly.

What the fuck does that mean?

"I thought you knew ... She's not interested in men, or boys for that matter. She's a lesbian, Ivy."

I gasped, and not because my daughter's sexual preference made a difference to me but because she hadn't told me. And worst of all, how could I not know?

Aren't mothers supposed to know these things?

My mind rolled back the film. How many times had I asked her about boys? How selfish could I be? Everyday questions I never considered: Are there any boys that you like in your class? Did any boys ask you to the dance? The boys are being nice to you, aren't they?

How stupid I've been, how out of the loop ...

"We should have told you about the class, but I just assumed she already had or would once she decided to commit to it fully. I promise you, she's not sexually active.

Not with anyone. And I'll ask her about the photo, but I'm basically certain that it's for an art project," Samantha was rambling now.

My head was spinning and my heart hurt. I wish Delaney would talk to me about these things, not Samantha. But at least she felt comfortable telling someone ...

"Ivy, are you still there?"

I cleared my throat. "I am. Thanks for clearing that up for me. It's a relief, honestly. I appreciate it. Talk to you later."

Samantha started to say something else, but I hung up the phone before I could hear it.

Chapter 11

BEFORE

"You know what they say. You have to get back in the saddle again ..." Pam teased.

We were talking about Ben again, but in truth, my mind was stuck on Delaney. Should I ask her about being gay, or wait for her to come to me?

Part of me wanted to tell her that I'd talked to Samantha and explain that I knew. I wanted to ask questions, to tell her I supported her no matter what ...

It wasn't the news I'd been expecting, but it was a huge relief. My daughter wasn't receiving creepy pictures from anyone, and she, hopefully, wasn't sexually active yet.

"Are you even listening?" Pam leaned over and flicked my ear like a childish school chum.

"Yeah ..."

"Seriously! Get on there and find someone to hook up with tonight. It'll help you get over Ben."

"You think I should try to message him again?" I asked, thinking back on the last several messages I'd already sent. I'd tried to make them sound casual, but as I'd read them back last night, they'd stunk of desperation.

"Absolutely not," Jerry cut in, carrying a stack of papers over to the copier. "If you do, I'll personally come over to your house and disable your account. I still have the password, you know."

Pam chimed in, "Jerry's right, honey. We don't chase ..."

But my mind was still on Jerry's words. I hadn't changed the password yet. *Stupid me.*

I didn't think he'd have the nerve or the audacity or the *desire* to log in and read my messages on there, but if he did ...

Now, that would be embarrassing.

"This whole dating thing is stupid," I said, reminding myself to log in and update the password as soon as I got home.

"It's not. It's fun. And it's necessary." Pam was still talking, but I drowned out the rest of the words as I shoved a pencil in the sharpener.

"I don't think it's *necessary*, per se," Jerry pondered over the grinding noise. "But a social life is important. It's good to have people to hang out with ..."

Pam was nodding in agreement, but she wasn't looking at me. She was staring at Jerry with this wanting look on her face a look full of desire. Jerry didn't seem to notice.

I wanted to ask him who he hung out with in his spare time, but I bit my tongue. His love life wasn't my business. And frankly, mine wasn't his either.

"Pick someone you can have some fun with. A one-night stand, perhaps?" Pam suggested, pulling her eyes away from Jerry and zeroing back in on me.

"Yeah, maybe I will," I lied.

***

Another late night where I couldn't sleep. Another shitty frozen meal in bed.

Delaney was still at her father's. I wanted to call her, tell her I missed her, ask her how she was feeling, beg her to open up, apologize for my role in the food fight ... but I let it be.

Ben still hadn't texted or called, and I'd avoided the dating site for days. But Pam's words circled back: *'pick someone you can have some fun with'.*

I shoved the plastic container of food and several bottles of beer aside and sauntered over to my computer desk. I logged into my account, a small, desperate part of me still hoping Ben might have messaged me here instead of on my cell.

There were no messages from Ben. And the status on his profile revealed he hadn't logged on in days.

Bummer.

No messages from him, but there were definitely ones from other guys – and a few attractive girls, too.

When Pam suggested a one-night stand, as much as I hated to admit it, one of the guys I'd friended online came to mind. MaxLove1985.

I'd looked at his profile a dozen times, and I scanned through his pictures again. He was shirtless in all of them. Shirtless Max in Cabo. Shirtless Max driving a boat. Shirtless Max lifting a sledgehammer. He was a construction worker, and in his mid-thirties and although he'd messaged me dozens of times already, I'd only responded twice. Not because I wasn't attracted to him, but because his boldness made me blush.

He'd already sent a couple naked photos to my inbox. *'Something to pleasure yourself with, baby.'*

He was young and athletic. Handsome and muscular in that ridiculous way some men are. I'd never been drawn to that type – always searching for someone a little more flawed, a little more vulnerable. Someone like me.

I imagined Max (if that was even his real name) sending out mass dick-pics to every woman on that list.

I took a long chug of my lukewarm beer and typed out a message, trying not to eyeball the nudes above in the messenger box ...

Hey. How are you?

It was totally lame, but what the hell else could I say? This man – all these guys – were ultimately strangers. I'd never been much good at small talk.

Max's response came through immediately.

Hi, beautiful! I'm working out naked.

I ran to the kitchen and grabbed another beer. I took a few nervous sips before letting my fingers hover over the keys.

What should I say?

Talking to guys like Ben and Richard had been easy because those were normal conversations. Max was another breed entirely ... your quintessential douchebag, just looking for hook-ups and fun.

Exactly what Pam thinks I need.

Before I could think up something good to say, a new picture came through.

Shirtless Max with a dumbbell. I rolled my eyes, but I had to admit he was handsome.

His next message read:

Want to see my lower half?

Surprising myself, I wrote back:

Sure. Why not?

It was stupid. Childish. But I was a little turned on, and I did sort of want to see the rest of him ...

A few minutes passed and I could feel myself growing in anticipation. The next thing that came through wasn't his lower half, as promised, but a self-invite.

Let me come over and I'll show you in person.

My cheeks flaming, I finished off my beer and crushed the can flat on my cherry oak desktop. Before I could change my mind, I typed out my address and clicked send.

Seconds later he had responded:
See you soon xoxo.

I stared at those words, that childlike abbreviation for hugs and kisses from my youth and suddenly, a memory I hadn't allowed myself to think about in months, came rushing back at me like a tidal wave, thick and all-encompassing.

Chapter 12

1993 – Andrea

*C-ya tonight. xoxoxoxoxoxoxoxoxoxoxoxoxoxoxoxoxoxoxo
xoxoxox*

There were so many x's and o's, just looking at them made me dizzy.

They had a plan – a crazy, evil plan. With me at the center of it.

When I'd heard Tamara and Mandy whispering in the toilet stall, I'd tucked my feet up to my chest, biting down on my kneecap to keep myself quiet. I don't know what I was listening for – a secret, sure. But something silly or sultry, like losing their virginities or who was cheating on who.

I was partially correct: they were gossiping about who was sleeping with who ... but the who's were what surprised me. And the second part scared me to death.

"It's true. All of it. Beck got it all on camera. If not for that, I never would have believed it ..." Mandy hissed.

"But this makes no sense. I'm not surprised about Jake – no offense. He's always been an asshole. But I never thought, not in a million years, that Philomena would fuck your man," Tamara said.

My stomach clenched at the sound of her name ... and at that forbidden word: *fuck*.

I'd heard my uncle say it countless times, and a few kids from school used it to show off for their friends. But Tamara and Mandy were talking about *sex*.

Did Philomena really sleep with Jake? I wondered.

If I'd have seen Jake on the street, I wouldn't have known him from Adam. I just knew *of* him. Jake Hawthorne was the high-school bad boy that somehow, some way, Mandy had managed to bag even though we were still in middle school. Mandy's older sister, who I also only knew through legend, went to high school with him. Mandy was always bragging about her older boyfriend – I don't know why everyone cared, but they did.

"Have you confronted her yet?" Tamara asked. "If not, you need to march out there and do it right now ..."

"No, no ... not now. You already know I'm more patient than that."

Something about the way she said it made the hairs on the back of my neck stand up.

"Why the hell not? Aren't you angry? I don't think I could pretend to be her friend for one more day if I were you.

I mean, you loved him, Mandy. You were saving yourself for him. And that bitch went and fucked up everything!" Tamara pressed her.

"I *still* love him. I'll never stop. And, hell yes, I'm angry. In fact, I'm angry enough to kill her."

For what felt like minutes, silence hovered in the gloomy bathroom. I held my breath, cheeks reddening.

They might kill me too, if they find out I'm listening in.

"I'll help you if you do," Tamara said, giving my heart a tiny jolt.

"That's what I hoped you would say," Mandy said, and I could hear the toothy, sly smile in her voice even though I couldn't see her. "But when? When can we teach her a lesson?"

Stunned, I listened with bated breath as they bounced around a few ideas: Briar Park, the old forestry, somewhere at school ...?

"No, none of those will work. That's how people get caught, stupid. We need to do it somewhere private, like one of our houses. A scene we can control ..." Mandy sounded faraway in thought, probably imagining herself killing the beautiful, backstabbing Philomena ...

"And a scene we can clean up after," Tamara whispered.

This time I couldn't help it; my body shivered involuntarily. I didn't think I'd made any sound, but the next thing I knew, I heard the stall door bang against the wall. A pair of tall black boots came stomping over and stopped right in front of my door.

"Who's in there?"

I froze as Mandy started banging on the door to my stall.

"Open up right now!" she commanded.

Sighing, I uncurled my legs and, nervously, I did just as she said, unlatching the door and creaking it open to look through.

Mandy looked angry, feet spread apart and hands mashed down on her hips. She was almost as pretty as Philomena herself ... *almost*.

Tamara came creeping out of the large stall at the end. Her face was white as a ghost.

"Did you hear anything we were saying?" she asked, her voice small and shaky.

"Every bit," I said, not taking my eyes off Mandy.

Mandy glanced over at Tamara. A silent exchange occurred between them. They were afraid of what I might do, of who I might tell.

"And? What are you going to do about it?" Mandy asked.

I took a deep breath, then said, "I know the perfect place. My uncle's house. He's never there. He's always working at the toothpaste factory. We could plan a slumber party on one of the nights he works super late. And I live in the middle of nowhere. We'd have all the privacy you could possibly need ..."

Mandy looked me up and down, assessing my worth.

Finally, she said, "Awesome," and shrugged. She motioned for Tamara to follow her out of the bathroom.

They stopped at the door, looking back at me. I was

glued to my place, standing at the doorway of my stall. I gripped the frame, trying not to faint at my own suggestion.

Was I this jealous of Philomena? Jealous enough to help with her murder?

"We'll be in contact soon," Mandy warned.

"But you don't know my house number ..."

"I don't need it. I'll leave you a note with instructions and dates. Put a check next to the day that works for you, when your uncle's working. I'll stick it in your locker. It won't be signed. Just lots of x's and o's. That's how you'll know it's me ..."

I swallowed down the lump in my throat as they exited the bathroom side by side. The door banged shut and I yelped.

"I'll be ready," I whispered, staring across the room at my own reflection in the row of sink mirrors. I almost didn't recognize myself.

Chapter 13

NOW

My body was hit with a tremor I hadn't felt in ages. The pills rattled in my hands. Slowly, I sat the bottles down, one by one, on the marble countertop, the name of its owner blurring ...

For a split second, I considered twisting the cap off one of the anti-anxiety medications and downing them all. Anything to get this old tremor to go away, anything to stop the horror erupting from under my skin.

But I don't have time for that.

These prescriptions didn't belong to Robin Regal. Which meant that either he didn't really live here – *could the address on his registration be wrong?* – or that he had a roommate.

A roommate I knew all too well.

I have to get out of here. It isn't safe ...

And right on cue, I heard the dull thwack of a car door slamming. I bolted out of the bathroom and darted through the apartment. I stopped in front of the bedroom window, eyes desperately scanning below.

A dark black truck with tinted windows was parked behind the Camaro. I watched in horror as the headlights popped off and the engine stopped.

Someone climbed out of the driver's seat. They were wearing a hood so dark I could barely see the outline of their face as they circled the Camaro, squatting down to look inside.

But I didn't need to see.

I knew.

Still, there was a desperate part of me that hoped – *prayed* – that my fears would be unfounded.

It's you. I know it is …

Chapter 14

BEFORE

I stared at my reflection in the bathroom mirror, eyes unblinking, lips parted in a troubled O.

Is this really what I look like now?

My hair was disheveled, my makeup from last night smudged beneath my eyes like a football player gearing up to run on the field. I was wearing only a t-shirt – not *my* t-shirt, I noted – and my panties.

Where did I toss them when I yanked them off in excitement?

Turning the faucet on, I began scrubbing my face. Brushing my teeth. Trying to wash the feel of Max away ...

He hadn't been rough, per se. But something about fucking him, this random guy, this ... *stranger,* made me feel dirty and used.

But you used him too, remember?

I dropped my toothbrush back into its holder and wiped the pasty residue from my mouth and chin.

I stared at my messy makeup and wild hair, my eyes wide. Then my face broke into a smile. I'd been another person in the bedroom, someone wild and free ... The alcohol had helped loosen me up, but it was mostly me. As dirty as it felt, it kind of felt good, too.

Maybe part of it was knowing that I'd never see this handsome stranger again.

Truth was, I hadn't actually thought Max would show. By the time he did, I was already buzzing from the nervous shots I'd taken, and unsure how to handle myself.

But Max had known what to do. He didn't ask questions, or show me pictures of his kids or dogs; he didn't blab about his latest ATV project ... He grabbed me around the waist and went straight to work kissing and groping, wriggling me out of my jeans.

"The bedroom. Not here," I'd panted, pulling him toward my room. Even though I was a little drunk and dizzy, I still knew I couldn't sleep with this man in the middle of the living room.

What if Delaney suddenly decided to come home?

So, to the bedroom we went, and there we stayed until nearly one in the morning. When we finished, I was sweating and breathless, my body limp from exhaustion ...

"That was fun, Amy."

I'd giggled at the name, but I didn't bother correcting him.

"Yeah it was, Mark," I'd replied, trying to keep my face straight. If he'd heard me, he didn't let on.

He was sitting on the end of my bed, his muscular back glistening with sweat. He stood up, stumbling around for his pants, and I watched him in amusement.

"Is it okay if I don't stay the night? I have some shit to do tomorrow," he said, buttoning his jeans. He retrieved a shiny black cell phone from his pocket, smiling a little as he swiped through his messages.

Another hook-up, perhaps? A few naughty messages from one of our fellow members on the dating site?

Either way, I didn't care. I didn't want him to stay the night, and frankly it was a relief to see him go.

"No problem. I have stuff to do, too." I rolled over on my side, reaching for my own phone while he tugged on his socks and laced up his Nikes. Still naked, I could feel him staring at my backside.

"Thanks for having me."

"Yeah, you too," I yawned. "Do you mind letting yourself out? I'm sleepy."

He smiled and raised one eyebrow in amusement.

"No probs. Well, I'll talk to you again soon. Hopefully."

"Yeah. Sure thing."

I lay on my side, listening to his soft footsteps until I heard the front door close behind him.

It felt good, not caring if someone left me for once …

Now here I stood, staring at the stranger in the mirror before me. I felt slightly dirty and guilty, but then again, I really didn't.

I'm a grown woman, and I'm single. I can do what I want.

I waltzed back to my room, then allowed myself to fall back on my cool bedsheets. I was tired, but I was also strangely wired, as though my body had come alive ...

I texted Pam, giving her a few of the dirty details. Then I fell back to sleep, letting the heady smell of sex and sweat lull me away ...

***

Sounds of a phone ringing jarred me out of bed. My fingers scrambled for it in the dark, but the place where I normally kept it on the nightstand was empty.

I struggled to open my eyes; they were clouded with sleep and my head was throbbing with pain. I'd gone back to sleep, but what time is it now?

The phone stopped ringing, then started again.

I forced myself to sit up, digging around in the covers until my fingers made contact with the plastic case.

"Hello?" my voice was raw and scratchy.

"Where are you?"

"Fuck!" It was then that I realized sunlight was seeping through my curtains, birds chirping outside. The only time I heard the birds or saw the early morning sun was on the weekends.

I'm late for work.

"Did you oversleep?" Pam asked, a flicker of amusement in her tone.

"Yeah. What time is it?"

"8:45."

"Holy shit! Cover for me, okay? Tell Bruce I had a flat tire, or something ..."

Pam lowered her voice. "He's not even in yet. He had an early meeting at the Balt House. If you hurry up, he won't even know."

"Okay. Bye." I hung up and leapt from the bed. In a frenzy, I shimmied into a black dress and heels.

Seeing myself in the mirror again, I remembered my strange encounter last night. Now, it felt like a dream, the details of my late-night escapade with Max fuzzy around the edges.

I quickly brushed my teeth and put on deodorant, but my hair ... nothing could tame this mess.

I twisted it into a knot at the base of my skull, skipped makeup, and ran for the van.

Thank goodness Delaney wasn't here or she probably would have missed the bus, I chastised myself as I slapped it into reverse and hit the gas.

There was a loud thump and the van jerked as I slammed into something.

"Oh my God!"

I put the van in park and jumped out, a hundred percent sure I'd hit my own trashcans. They often got knocked around by the wind, and today, I didn't even look behind me to make sure the driveway was clear of them.

As I ran around the back of the van, I immediately knew I'd hit more than a mailbox. There was a painful moan, and that's when I saw her.

My neighbor, Fran, slumped on the ground behind my left tire.

Chapter 15

BEFORE

"Fran!"

This can't be happening. This can't be happening. This can't be freaking happening!

"Uhhh ..." Fran's eyes fluttered open, then, much to my dismay, she started lifting her head off the ground.

"No, don't do that! Don't move. I'll call for an ambulance."

I don't remember what I said next – the words were jumbled, one long string of pleas. A voice not even my own begged someone to help on the other end of the line.

I knelt back down beside Fran. Her eyes were still open, wide and wary.

There's no blood. She can't be dying if there's no blood, right?

"Does anything feel broken?" I gently placed my fingers on her arm, feeling for what, I wasn't sure. Fran was moving her legs, trying to sit up, so they weren't broken then. But her arm ... her right arm was twisted at a funny angle.

My stomach curled in on itself as I stared at an edge of bone sticking out.

"Stop trying to move, please. I think your right arm might be broken. An ambulance is on its way. It'll all be okay, I promise ..."

"Quit talking to me like I'm a child," Fran snapped.

"I'm sorry," I said, quietly. "I didn't see you! What were you doing in my driveway anyway?"

"Your mail. Wrong box ..." Fran huffed. That was when I saw it — several envelopes scattered around the yard, blowing away with the wind ...

"I'm so sorry," I repeated.

Fran rolled her eyes, still facing her head away from me. That arm was looking mighty nasty, and I fought back the urge to vomit.

Sirens rose in the distance, a welcome relief.

"There they are. Almost here ..."

"Nothing is wrong with my damn ears," Fran snapped.

Moments later, the ambulance whipped around the corner, and pulled up next to the curb. Two young paramedics climbed out.

"What happened here?" one shouted, as the other began unloading a stretcher from the back.

"I hit my neighbor with my van. She was bringing me mail," I said, dully.

"Step back, please." I did as I was told, watching with

concern as one of the paramedics sat on the ground beside Fran and began assessing her injuries.

Fran still looked pissed off, but she surprised me by saying, "Young man, this was my fault. I walked right in front of her while she was backing out. A total accident."

"No, Fran. I should have looked ..."

The paramedic glanced back at me, briefly, and then Fran said to me: "Do you ever stop talking, lady?"

I pursed my lips and leaned against the back of the van.

I definitely wasn't going to make it into work before my boss showed up. I needed to call the office, but it seemed rude to take out my cell phone with Fran still sprawled out on the ground.

"This arm does look broken."

The other paramedic joined him with a stretcher in tow.

"I don't need that. My legs are fine. I can walk myself over," Fran said. Once again, she tried to sit up, but the young paramedic held her down.

"There could be more broken bones. Or worse, internal injuries. The doctors will have to look and see."

"I'll ride with you," I said, gently.

"No, you won't," Fran huffed, just as I heard more sirens.

"Ma'am, you'll need to stay here. The police will need to speak with you," the young man said. My heart lurched.

As they loaded Fran into the ambulance, a police officer arrived on the scene. I prayed that I'd done a good enough job of brushing my teeth this morning, because four hours ago, I was hammered drunk.

Chapter 16

BEFORE

The next day it was front page news:
ELDERLY WOMAN RUN DOWN BY NEIGHBOR

"Christ!" I slapped the newspaper shut and pinched the bridge of my nose as hard as I could.

"They make it sound like I ran her down on purpose. A maniac running down a sweet old lady in the street ..." I moaned.

I expected Pam to laugh or make a joke, to tell me to stop being so dramatic. But she reached for me, pulling me in for a hug.

We were sitting at my kitchen table, untouched coffees beside us.

I let her hold me, enjoying the sweet smell of her coconut shampoo and the tickle of her dyed blonde hair on my cheek as I swallowed down the lump in my throat that always appeared when I was on the verge of tears.

Finally, she released me, but gripped both of my shoulders with her hands. She gave me a determined look.

I know that look.

"This could have been so much worse. We both know how much worse She could have been killed, Ivy. And it was an honest mistake. I can't tell you how many times I've backed up in my own driveway without a second thought. When you live alone and don't have small pets or kids, you don't always think about what's behind you ..."

But that's the thing: I usually do. It's just that on that particular morning, I had been over-tired and hungover. Still possibly a little drunk.

Luckily for me, Fran wasn't pressing charges. Her arm was broken and I'd offered to pay her medical bills.

Who was I kidding? I didn't have money for that.

But she'd assured me that she had insurance and I needn't worry. The cop who'd taken the report had also been kind. They hadn't asked me if I'd been drinking and they hadn't carted me off to jail ...

The only people who seemed upset with me were the people who were supposed to love me the most: my daughter and her father. I'd called Michael first to tell him about the accident, not because I wanted to share, or because he cared, but because I didn't want him hearing it from someone else. Or seeing it on the front of today's paper.

"You always were a shitty driver," he said, the disgust evident in his voice.

I wonder if he called Samantha a 'shitty driver' when she had her accident.

I'd expected Delaney to call after he told her, but I still hadn't heard a word. I guess an accident involving me didn't require the sort of tearful reaction that Samantha's wreck did.

But that's unfair. Samantha's accident hadn't been her fault, and she'd been injured. This time, it's the other way around …

"I don't know, Pam …" I reached for the paper, begrudgingly turning it over, then back. The picture of me was terrible – double chin, teary-eyed, hair a mess. I was carrying a bouquet of cheap flowers in my hand, crossing the hospital parking lot to visit Fran.

Someone had snapped the photo of me, apparently. I wished I'd seen them do it. I would have slapped their phone from their hands.

And gotten in even more trouble.

"What don't you know?" She picked up her mug of coffee and blew steam off the top.

"I mean, you'd think they'd have something better to do than reporting on this story. I just can't believe how bad this makes me look …"

"Exactly!" Pam huffed. "It's not like you did it on purpose, or like you were drinking and driving."

"Well …" For a split second, I considered telling the truth – about the late-night sex with Max, about how I'd gotten so drunk that I'd passed out and forgot to re-set my alarm, about how it never occurred to me that I was probably still a little intoxicated, having only drunk a few hours earlier ...

"Well, what?" Pam urged, her eyes searching mine worriedly. She took a sip of her coffee, eyes watching me curiously over the cup.

"I was up too late with this guy I met online. I was tired, not thinking straight ..."

"Oh, I know. You texted me at like four in the morning, remember?"

Actually, I'd forgotten. "Sorry about that," I said, meekly.

"Don't be. You deserve to have fun, Ivy. Don't beat yourself up. Fran's going to be okay, and from now on, you'll be more careful when you're backing up."

"Yeah." I took a long, hot sip of my own coffee, enjoying the brutal burn on my tongue.

I fucked up – simple as that.

Because of me, an old lady was injured. She could have been killed.

I wish I could say it's the worst thing I've ever done, but that would be a lie ...

Chapter 17

1993 – Andrea

For a moment, I could almost imagine that this was my *real* life: me and my three best friends, hanging out in my bedroom on a Friday night.

"What do you think?" Philomena asked, smiling down at my nails. She seemed so calm, so unaware ...

"They're beautiful," I said honestly. They were. Normally, when I tried to paint my own nails, my hands shook with a nervous tremor, the paint messy, always outside the lines.

"You should have her do your eyebrows next. Philomena is an expert when it comes to personal grooming," Mandy said. She was staring at me from where she sat cross-legged on the floor, eyes narrowed.

I know that look.

It's time. Time for the plan to be carried out ...

"Do you mind? I have tweezers in my bathroom. It's kind

of cramped and gross in there but the lighting's good." My words were shivery little whispers in the silent room.

"Sure," Philomena said, flashing that lovely, bright smile of hers. As I followed her to the bathroom, a short walk that felt strangely endless, I glanced over my shoulder at Mandy and Tamara.

Tamara held up three fingers and mouthed something. "Remember what to do," I thought she said.

I stepped inside the bathroom, closing the door behind me.

Philomena was already digging in my off-track sink drawers, looking for the tweezers.

Three fingers meant three minutes.

Three minutes before Philomena's friends planned to kill her.

Chapter 18

NOW

For a moment, I was frozen in time, watching the hooded figure approaching the building.

Panicked, I turned around and ran for the stairs.

I have to get out of here. Now!

I raced down the steps, leaping over the last half dozen, and sliding across the landing like a summer slip 'n' slide.

I heard a low chime – the bell on the front door ringing as someone walked in. Someone with a key.

I burst through the back door, the cold night air smacking me in the face the greatest sensation in the world.

I didn't have a car to drive home in. All I have is my own two feet.

Instead of running around the building to the main road, I charged straight through the alley and cut through dozens of yards, side-stepping garden gnomes and leaping through hedges.

By the time I stopped, I'd gone nearly a mile in the wrong direction from home.

I panted, turning around in circles, looking for any signs that I'd been followed.

But there was no one there. The only sound was the cool brush of tired leaves falling like snow from the sky. Bending over, I placed my hands on my kneecaps as I struggled to catch my breath.

I was on a residential street, one I'd seen before but didn't know the name of. The houses were old but well cared for, neat whimsical designs and wraparound porches. They reminded me of miniature versions of Michael's pretty new monster house.

Most of the houses were dark but a few were lit up. Carved pumpkins and cheap plastic skeletons adorned a few of the porches, even though it wasn't Halloween yet.

I stepped onto the sidewalk, digging my phone out of my pocket. I used my Uber app to schedule a ride.

Next, I dialed a number, looking all around me to make sure no one was sneaking up from behind or beside me ...

"Hello?"

I cleared my throat, then said the words I had hoped I'd never have to say: "It's me. Listen, he's back. He wants revenge for what we did," I said, breathlessly.

Chapter 19

BEFORE

The pie pan burned the tips of my fingers, but I didn't flinch, determined to endure whatever discomfort the fates delivered upon me. As I crossed the street, I glanced left and right to make sure no one was watching – or snapping photos of me this time.

I walked the hot cherry pie up the flagstone walkway that led to Fran's front door.

The front lights were out, the curtains drawn, but her Oldsmobile was parked in the driveway. I prayed she wasn't sleeping.

Balancing the pie in one hand, I knocked softly with the other.

I couldn't bake for shit, so I'd bought one of those pre-made pies that you warm up for thirty minutes. Surely, she wouldn't know the difference, would she?

Knowing my luck, she's probably diabetic.

The door swung open with an irritated bang. Fran stood there in a ratty old gown. Her right arm snug in a plain white cast.

"I'm so sorry, Fran."

She groaned and threw up her good hand in disgust. "You didn't come here to apologize repeatedly, did you? You did that in the driveway, then at the hospital, then when I got home ... Please just stop. I know you're sorry already. After a while, I get sick of hearing it ..."

"Okay. I'll stop saying it." I held out the pie, an apology in its own right.

"I only got one good hand," Fran said, dully, loosely shaking her good left arm.

"Oh." My cheeks were flaming.

"It's alright, don't get all weepy on me again. Just carry it in and put it over there on the table for me." She stepped aside and motioned with her head for me to come in.

I'd expected Fran's house to look like a carbon copy of mine, but it was older, wallpaper with dizzying swirl designs papering her living room wall. Her furniture was old, but sturdy. There was a blue love seat with flowery cushions and a lazy boy chair. But what I noticed most was that there were books everywhere. Books lining the shelves on both sides of the room. Books stacked on the coffee table and end tables. Even stacks of books on the floor.

"Wow. You must love to read," I said, impressed.

"A regular Sherlock Holmes, aren't ya? Kitchen's in here."

I followed her, passing through the dining room which contained a large table littered with more books, and entered the kitchen.

The sink and counters were covered in dirty dishes.

"Excuse my mess. It's kind of hard to wash with one hand. Jim tried to talk me into getting a dishwasher for years, but I was too stubborn. Should have listened to that old fool."

"Who's Jim?" I scooted a few of the dishes over, making room for the pie.

"My husband. He's been dead for a decade. Heart attack."

"I'm so sorry."

Fran grunted. "You promised not to say that again."

"Oops. I am, though. That must have been difficult for you." I started opening and closing drawers, looking for a good knife to slice with.

"Why don't you sit down and let me bring you a piece of pie? Rest that arm of yours," I suggested.

I expected her to protest, but she simply grunted and walked over to a small two-person dinette. I watched her struggle to pull out the chair one handed.

I thought about Samantha with her neck brace. "How long until the cast comes off?"

Carefully, I sliced the pie and started looking around for a couple clean plates.

"Six weeks at the very least."

There weren't any clean plates I could see. I filled the sink with hot water and dish soap, scrubbed off one of the plates and carried it over to her with two slices of pie and a fork balanced on it.

She grumbled something that might have been "thank you".

I started loading the sink with dishes while she picked at the pie.

A few minutes later, she said, "Who on earth taught you how to bake?"

I rolled my eyes. "No one. My mom and dad died when I was young. I got it from the store." I started to apologize again, but she shot me a look: *don't you dare.*

"How about you? Have any family?" I asked tentatively, as I started scrubbing.

"None that matter."

I wanted to ask more but didn't. Fran had to be at least eighty years old. I'd originally guessed seventy but seeing her up close ... her skin was paper thin, her face webbed with deep crinkles and lines.

Even without a broken arm, I couldn't imagine what it must feel like to be alone all the time in this house.

"Do you miss your husband?" I asked, struggling to dislodge a dried clump of jelly off one of the plates.

"Do you miss yours?" Fran snapped back. She picked up her fork and stabbed the pie repeatedly.

"Not a bit," I lied, giving her a sideways smile. "I didn't know you knew I was married. My ex rarely comes to the house."

"Well, I didn't know. And I don't care, really. But I figured someone had to be responsible for fathering that girl of yours."

I don't know why, but her words cut me to the core.

That girl of yours.

I could handle people being rude to me – it comes with the territory when you work in sales.

But no one, and I mean no one, gets to talk shit about my child.

"What does that mean?" I set down the glass I'd been washing and dried off my hands.

Fran shrugged, then flinched in pain, reaching tenderly to rub her arm.

"What do you have against my daughter?" I crossed my arms and leaned against the counter, waiting. "It seems like you've hated us since we moved in."

"Hate. Now that's an ugly word. I don't hate you, or your daughter," Fran sniffed. "It's just ..."

"Just what?"

"After a while, I got used to being alone. It felt like I had this whole God-awful place to myself. No one ever moved in; the place went belly-up, I guess ... and after Jim died, it was hard. But then, I kind of got used to things. I don't hate you; I just don't like having any neighbors."

My heart softened a bit.

She's a sad woman, I realized.

I could see it in her eyes, which were clouded over with pain. They reminded me of my own eyes, heavy and sad after my mom and dad passed ...

"I understand that," I said, softly. "But it's not like we play loud music or—"

"Run me down with your car." Fran wiggled her eyebrows, then surprised me by snorting with laughter. "Seriously though, you all are pretty good neighbors. But I have trouble sleeping and all-night visitors don't help."

My stomach flipped with regret.

Is she talking about my recent rendezvous with Max?

"I rarely have any guests over. Sometimes my friend Pam comes by, or one of Delaney's friends drops her off after school ... and I've only had one late-night visitor, recently. I'm a grown woman. I'm allowed to—"

"That's not what I'm talking about."

"I don't understand," I said, feeling myself growing angry again.

"For weeks, there's been a truck out there every night. Black, dark tinted windows. Although, I haven't seen it in a couple days, now that I mention it ..."

I shook my head, confused. What in the world is she talking about?

"He shows up around two in the morning and just sits out there. It makes me uneasy. I figured it was a friend of your daughter's. Maybe a boyfriend."

I was still shaking my head. If someone was parking outside our house every night, surely Delaney or I would have noticed ...

My thoughts returned to the naked photo messages.

143

Samantha said it was for an art project, but what if she was wrong? What if Delaney had a stalker?

Or could it be someone looking for me?

Maybe someone who knows the truth about my past.

Chapter 20

1993 – Andrea

Streaks of brown and orange mildew lined the walls of my uncle's bathroom. I thought I'd pulled the shower curtain shut before the girls came over, but when I followed Philomena inside, it was pushed all the way to the right-hand side.

Black scabs of mold gathered in the corners. Flecks of my uncle's brown-gray beard congregated by the drain.

Philomena, who didn't seem to mind the mess, sat down on the edge of the tub. Her chocolate-brown eyes were quiet and serious. I sat on the closed toilet seat and stared back.

Three minutes. Probably only two by now …

"Let's get started then." Philomena stood up and clicked the tiny tweezers at me, teasingly.

Too fast. The clocking is winding down too quickly …

There was a bang on the bathroom door. I knew it had to be Mandy.

"Open up! Something's wrong with Tamara. I think she's going to be sick!"

I couldn't move. I was frozen on my porcelain throne.

But Philomena didn't hesitate. She stepped forward and unbolted the door to let them in.

I sprang to life, moving aside and lifting the heavy lid for Tamara.

Tamara wasn't sick. This was part of the plan.

Tamara knelt on the floor in front of the commode. She started making these awful retching noises ...

Mandy squeezed into the bathroom too, locking the bathroom door behind her.

"Are you okay, girl?" Philomena looked over at Tamara who was hunched down by the commode, heaving.

While Philomena and Tamara were distracted, Mandy gave me a wide-eyed knowing look. I nodded that I understood.

Squatting down in front of the filthy sink, I opened the lower cabinet doors. Beside the exposed plastic tubing, the knife lay steely in the dark.

I picked it up, fingers folding easily around the grip, which was wrapped tightly with thick black tape. My uncle used it for skinning fish sometimes.

Today, its use would be much more sinister.

Chapter 21

NOW

There once was a time when I craved silence. The kind of silence you just can't get ...

When Delaney was little, Michael and I took her to The Caverns, a cheap fun park that featured a manmade cave tour and chunky bags of gravel you could sift through, looking for gemstones. If you paid a little extra, they guaranteed a certain number of "treasures".

That entire day at The Caverns was a blur now ... it was so long ago. But what I do remember is the cave tour and the silence. It involved climbing onto a boat and our tour guide drove us through shallow water to see stalagmites, stalactites, and bones dating back to the Ice Age.

"Now, I want everyone to stay quiet. Don't talk, don't move ... then I'm going to turn off my light, so you all can experience what it feels like to be in utter darkness down here.

When the lights went out, it *was* dark – eerily so. But what struck me the most wasn't the dizzying tunnel of darkness; it was the silence. Even in an empty house or empty field, you couldn't achieve that sort of quiet. There were always sounds – thunder, birds chirping, refrigerators running, pipes groaning – but down there, 110 feet underground, I experienced, for a few minutes, what absolute silence felt like.

And I craved it when Delaney was young.

There were times, as a young, inexperienced, still-grieving mother, that I closed my eyes and counted to ten, picturing myself all alone in that cave. Utter silence. Peace.

When the Uber driver dropped me off and I went in, the house was painfully quiet inside.

But there was nothing peaceful about it. Michael had moved on with his new wife and Delaney wasn't here either. Finally, I'd achieved the silence I'd always wanted.

But now it felt deafening, loud ... scary.

If I closed my eyes, I could conjure sounds, remnants of a life long gone, but not forgotten: the low murmur of Michael watching TV, Delaney dancing in the living room, her little legs punching the air as she practiced ballet steps; the smell of Michael's cologne, and the constant aroma of leftovers and day-old garbage ... a constant, flowing life.

Now the house felt stagnant. Empty.

And the truth was that I wasn't alone. Not at all. I was

sharing space with two dead bodies. And it wasn't only my secret anymore …

I've been found. Found out.

It was only a matter of time …

I checked every single lock in the house, on the windows and on the doors, then locked myself in my bedroom. The bodies were still laid out on the floor, but I'd covered them both with extra sheets. The bloody sheet from my bed was still wound up in the corner of my room.

And beside the bodies, the empty golf bags lay unused.

I have to make the call. There's no other choice.

My breath was still wheezy from my panicked bolt from Robin Regal's apartment.

So, it's finally happened. He's out of prison. And now he's come for revenge.

Chapter 22

BEFORE

"It's important that you tell me the truth."

My words hung in the air between us, another silent battle between Delaney and me. Another battle I'd probably soon lose ...

"I already did," Delaney huffed, crossing her arms over her chest. She leaned back against the couch cushions, raising her chin defiantly.

Your move, Mom.

"Yeah, she did," Michael parroted from beside her.

I released an internal groan.

How mature, and how stupid, of me to include him in this discussion.

Delaney had barely responded to my calls or texts, so I'd done what any sensible co-parent would do: I'd gone over her head and called her dad.

I'd told Michael about the mystery vehicle, the one Fran claimed she'd seen nearly every single night. Last night, I'd stood guard in the living room, watching from a crack in the blinds to catch him, or her, in the act.

But no vehicle had come. My first thought was that maybe Fran was wrong. But something in my gut told me she was right. Delaney was hiding something from me; I could feel it.

I've felt it for a while now, deep in my bones.

I ignored Michael's unhelpful response and said, "Listen, Laney. I don't care if you have a boyfriend. Or a girlfriend. And if you've been sneaking someone in or going out; you're not in trouble here. I just want to know the truth, because if it's not someone you know, then I'm worried you might have a stalker."

Delaney's face was beet red. She stared straight over my head, eyes watching the swish, swish, swish of the cat-tail clock on the wall.

Michael took her hand in his, the gesture surprising me and Delaney both.

"Your mom's just worried about you, honey. If you know who it is, tell her. If you don't, well ... tell her that, too. Just tell us the truth, honey. We want to make sure you're safe, that's all," he urged her.

I expected her to get angry with him, as she had done with me, but instead, her bottom lip quivered. She looked away, wiping at her eyes to cover the tears.

For a moment, I thought she was about to tell us

something important, but then, she said, "I already told you. I don't know who it is. Nobody's stalking me. Nobody's following me. Nobody knows I'm even alive!"

Her words cut me to the core.

"Laney ..."

She bolted from the couch and ran to her bedroom, slamming the door.

Michael and I stared at each other, unsure what to do next.

Finally, I spoke. "I'm going to contact the police and let them know what Fran saw. I'm concerned that this car hasn't been around the last few nights. Almost like he or she knows that Delaney hasn't been here. What if he's been watching her at your house? She's been staying there a lot lately."

Michael's face hardened. "Well, if he is, I can find out pretty fast. I have security cameras out front, facing the street, and ones in the back and on the sides of the house as well."

"Really?" This surprised me. I knew he could afford something like that, but why did he need it? It seemed a little ... intrusive. And I hadn't noticed any cameras the other day.

"Does Delaney know there are cameras?" I asked, quietly.

I couldn't hear her in her room, but I had a feeling she was standing on the other side of the door, listening.

"Of course she does," Michael snapped. "I'll go home and check the footage right away. But in the meantime, tone it down a bit, OK? You're upsetting her, and it's probably over nothing. Who's to say this old bag isn't just seeing things, or maybe she made it up? Old ladies are nosy like that …"

I rolled my eyes. Leave it to Michael to blame everyone else, and to make fun of my neighbor because of her age.

Michael stood up and smoothed the wrinkles from his suit.

"How's Samantha doing?" I asked, watching him pick at tiny balls of lint on his pants.

The house was messy, but for once I didn't care. I was too worried about my daughter to concern myself with Michael's snobbery.

"Fine. Why?" Once again, he seemed irritated by my voice.

Some things never change.

"Because she recently broke her neck. I was wondering if she was healing alright," I snapped back.

Michael mumbled something that sounded like, "She'll live," just as Delaney's door snapped open again. She had changed into her black and purple skull shirt and combed her hair back into a stubby black ponytail. For the second time in days, I was stunned by how thin she looked, nearly skull-like herself.

"Stop fighting, you two," she said, narrowing her eyes.

"We weren't," I said, but we all knew it was a lie.

Delaney was old enough to remember the words and the fights, the toxic relationship Michael and I once had.

Still have, I guess.

153

"Is it okay if I stay at Dad's for a couple more nights ... just till the weekend? Sam wants to take the twins to Chucky Cheese tonight. They've never been before. And I know she'll need my help with them ..."

"Why aren't you going?" I couldn't help it; I had to ask. I fixed my eyes on Michael.

"I have to go out of town for a couple days. We're working on a new deal in Oklahoma. I'm flying out tonight and coming back on Saturday."

So, technically, my daughter wasn't staying with her dad. She was staying with her stepmom. Another flare of jealousy sprang up, but I quickly tried to extinguish it. Delaney was old enough to decide where she wanted to stay now. And if there really was someone eye-spying our house, either watching her or me, then maybe it was better for her to be with her stepmom, where they were less isolated and had better security.

"That's fine, Laney."

I turned to Michael. "Before you leave, will you check out the camera footage and call me? I know it's probably nothing, but it would really put my mind at ease."

"Will do," Michael clipped. He wrapped an arm around Delaney's shoulders and led her toward the door. She looked uncomfortable with his touch, which gave me a glimmer of satisfaction.

At least I'm not the only one she can't stand, I thought.

Standing at the door, I watched them go. Michael pointed toward the passenger's seat, but Delaney shook her head and climbed in the backseat. I held back another smile.

I waved, even though neither were looking.

But as they pulled away, Delaney's eyes lifted and met mine. She stared out at me, her eyes big and sorrowful, and as the car rolled away from the curb, a memory came rushing back: the first time Michael took her, right after the divorce.

She'd have been only six or seven then, but unlike today, she hadn't looked sad at all. She'd been excited to go with her father, always aiming her anger and disappointment at me. For a moment, I'd had this crazy sensation that I might never see her again. Not because something bad was going to happen, but because she'd stop loving me. Just like her father did.

"I taught you how to tie your shoes," I had shouted after her that day. But it was windy, and the words blew back in my face.

For a moment, I thought there was no way she could have heard me, but then she'd leaned out of her open window and grumbled, "Love you too, Mom."

She had misheard my words for "I love you", which was probably for the best.

It was a strange thing to say, a strange thought to have ... but it was the truth. Michael was the fun one, the one who paid her little attention during the week because he was always working, but then rushed out to buy her the latest gadget or Barbie or whatever she wanted come the weekend.

It was me, unnoticed, doing the grunt work in the trenches. The cooking, the washing, the fighting over homework. The one who set down the rules. The one who punished her when those rules weren't followed.

She had always been a daddy's girl. When she was little, I had loved it. I enjoyed watching Michael swoop her into the air, those chubby little legs wrapping around his neck and shoulders, but I think I resented it then too. And maybe, deep down, I had always wondered … if Dillan had lived, would he have been a mama's boy?

I hated myself for wondering things like that.

"I taught you how to tie your shoes." I said the words again, clear and loud this time, but there was no one left to hear them anymore.

Chapter 23

1993 – Andrea

The knife steady in my hand, I took a step toward Philomena's backside. Mandy watched my approach, a toothy, mad smile blossoming across her face.

Philomena whipped around, eyes zeroing in on the knife I was wielding. She glanced down at it, perfectly aligned with her belly button, then looked up at me and smiled.

I turned the knife around and gave it to her, handle first.

"Going to kill me, were you? Oh wait, you were too much of a coward for that. Trying to make Andrea here do your dirty work."

Philomena poked the knife at Mandy's chest.

The fake-puking had stopped, and Tamara was struggling to get on her feet. Mandy looked from Philomena to me, then her lips curled into a snarl.

"I have no idea what you're talking about. Are you high?" Mandy asked. She released a nervous laugh, then reached for the door.

"Don't you dare move," Philomena hissed. The tip of the knife tore a small hole in Mandy's shirt. I took a step back from the girls, frightened.

"What are you going to do? Stab me?" Mandy didn't take her hand off the knob, but she held it still, eyes wide as she realized Philomena was serious.

"Were you really going to kill me, just because I slept with Jake? Do you know how insane, how evil, that is?"

"What's evil is a best friend who thinks it's okay to fuck any guy she wants. I loved him! And you went and screwed him anyway," Mandy cried.

Suddenly, Philomena lowered the knife, then sighed deeply. "I'm sorry, Mandy. I wanted to tell you afterwards. I was drunk and stupid, and I should have come straight to you, but he was so sad and regretful. He told me he loved you and hated himself for what he did. I figured that telling you would be worse."

"Oh, don't act like you care about her feelings now," Tamara said, squeezing between the two girls, obviously unafraid of the knife. "If you really gave a shit, you wouldn't have done it in the first place, Philomena!"

"Oh, shut up! You've always been jealous of me and you're always trying to turn Mandy against me," Philomena screamed. "But, talking her into killing me? Wow! That must have been a dream come true for you."

The bathroom was too hot. Too cramped. I was backed up against the railing of the tub. I leaned too far, desperately grabbing for the curtain to stop myself from falling.

But I fell anyway, pulling down the clear plastic curtain as I hit the tiles.

Philomena glanced back at the ruckus I was making, and when she did, Mandy lunged.

Like a slow-motion movie, I watched Mandy and Tamara wrestle Philomena to the ground. Tamara started kicking and punching with all her might and Mandy reached down for something on the ground ...

No!

When Mandy stood up, she was smiling, and I saw the knife gleaming mercilessly in her hand.

She was going to kill Philomena after all.

Still holding the ripped shower curtain in my hand, I ran straight for her, knocking her off balance. Once again, the knife hit the floor.

Somewhere in the background were grunts and groans – Tamara and Philomena scuffling for the knife ...

My focus was on Mandy. Her backside was rammed against the bathroom door, but she simply pushed off, gaining more momentum, and propelled herself straight for me. Before she could collide into me, I sidestepped left then swooped around, grabbing her from behind. I wrapped the plastic curtain over her face and squeezed with all might.

I thought about my mother and the jingle of her laughter

in the kitchen. My father and the smell of dusky old smoke at dawn. And then I thought about the stupid drunk driver who'd not only killed them, but who'd killed me that day too – a huge chunk of me gone with them, certainly the most important parts of me ...

And my uncle, so mean and menacing; I hated living with that freaking prick.

Mandy fought for her life, slamming her heels into my shins, even whipping her head around and clipping me so hard on the chin I thought I saw stars for a minute, but Mandy's fear was no match for my rage. I refused to let up or let go ...

I was still squeezing when her body went limp in my hands.

Two shaky hands grabbed me by the shoulders.

"Stop. You have to stop now, please." It was Philomena. When I turned to look at her, she was so pasty white that I almost didn't recognize her.

"For a moment, I forgot ... I forgot ..." I couldn't finish the sentence. The thought had become dislodged.

I let go of Mandy, watching her body slump to the floor, the see-through plastic curtain still covering her entire face.

"What did I do?"

"It's okay." Philomena forced me to look away, to turn around and face her instead. She wrapped her arms around me, drawing me in for a hug, repeating, "It's going to be okay. It's going to be okay; I promise ..."

And then she said, "You saved my life, Andrea. They

were going to kill me. If you hadn't told me beforehand, it'd be me dead on the floor, not them."

Them?

Over Philomena's shoulder, my eyes locked on another limp body on the ground. Tamara lay curled up next to the commode. She was facedown; blood spread out like a fan beneath her ...

Oh my God.

Moments earlier, Tamara was fake-puking and Mandy was snarling ... and before that, we were laughing and sitting around my living room ... and now two of them are dead.

They are dead.

Philomena squeezed me tighter and suddenly I realized I was sobbing, loudly and hysterically.

"What did we do?" I moaned.

"Look at me. Look. At. Me."

When I lifted my eyes to hers, I realized that hers were red and puffy, too. She was just as traumatized as I was.

"We did what we had to do. They were going to kill you. And when they found out I told you ... well, they probably would have killed us both," I said, trying to be the strong one now.

"I know ..." Philomena rubbed her face with her hands. She glanced over her shoulder at Tamara's body, at what she had done, and I swear her face turned green.

"We have to call the police. We have to tell them the truth about what happened," I told her.

"You know we can't do that. Think about those other girls in the news ..."

My mind drifted back to those other murders. A young girl, a few years older than us, brutally tortured and murdered by three of her peers. It had been a media circus, still all over the news a year later ...

"They'll never believe us," Philomena spoke softly, more to herself than to me. "They'll think we're cold-blooded killers, just like all the other kids you see every day in the news ..."

"But they have to. They have to."

"They won't," she said, firmly. "Life isn't fair. If it were, you wouldn't even be standing here, talking to me. You'd be home in Clarkton, with your mom and dad, not in this stupid trailer with your piece-of-shit uncle ..."

"Listen," I said, my mind made up. "You go on home. I'll take care of this. No one will ever have to know you were here. I'll tell them it was only me ..." But as the words flowed out, I knew they weren't true. Mandy's older sister had dropped off the girls. She knew Philomena had been with them ...

Come morning, Mandy and Tamara's parents would be calling or coming by to get them. There was no hiding what had happened here.

"I'm not leaving you to deal with this alone. No way," Philomena said, puffing out her chest. "Whatever we decide to do, we decide together. Just me and you, okay?"

Despite the horror surrounding me in the bathroom, I

felt a glimmer of hope shine through. It had been so long since I'd had a friend – a real one. Philomena was not only pretty and kind, she was brave too.

If I went to jail, I would lose that. I would lose her.

"I know what to do," I said, drawing her in close to share my plan.

Chapter 24

NOW

Two dead sparrows, black and blue.
One for the lady. One for you.

I couldn't remember where I'd heard the poem, but it came floating back like it'd never left my subconscious in the first place.

Two bodies on the floor in my uncle's trailer.

Two bodies in my bedroom now.

Only this time, I don't know how they got here. I didn't kill them ...

"Hello? Are you still there? Please answer me, Ivy."

The phone rested between my shoulder and cheek. The room spun, the shadows of the two dead bodies dancing on the walls like a cinema of macabre silhouettes.

I couldn't remember the year, but Delaney couldn't

have been much older than four or five. A had windstorm knocked all the power out, and it had taken nearly six days to fix it. Michael had been out of town, but we hadn't minded. We'd made shadow shows on the wall, and I'd told her stories – wild, elaborate, silly stories – and she'd laughed so hard that she'd peed the bed.

If only Delaney knew the truth. That her mother was a monster. A killer.

"Dammit, I hear you breathing! Talk to me. Say something."

I opened my mouth but only one word came out: "Philomena."

There was a small intake of breath on the other end.

"Please don't call me that." But she didn't sound angry, just sad.

"He's back."

"How do you know?" she asked, voice steady.

"Because I was just in his apartment," I whispered.

Chapter 25

BEFORE

I stared at the food on the table, slimy chicken and over-cooked potatoes displayed on a platter. Peas and carrots in a bowl. A package of store-bought rolls, unopened.

I said her name again, only quieter. "Delaney. Please come to dinner."

There was no point.

She's not coming.

It was her first night back in days. As usual, my hopes of how things would go varied greatly from reality. She'd been shut up in her room since I'd got home from work.

Sighing noisily so she could hear me (if she was even listening), I picked up my fork and stabbed a piece of chicken onto my plate. The potatoes were cold and mushy now. I scooted my plate up against the platter and swept a small lumpy pile of peas next to the chicken.

I had no appetite.

I was still worried about the late-night visitor, and I'd been staying up late every night to catch him, leaving me dead-dog tired when it came time to wake up and go into work. I hadn't called the cops, afraid of upsetting Delaney more, and looking hysterical in a town that already didn't think too highly of me.

And my boss wasn't happy — the recent article in the paper "reflected poorly on the company", according to him. I'd expected his next words to be, "We're letting you go." But that hadn't happened yet.

Fran had forgiven me, but everyone else was giving me side-eye looks, as though I'd hit the poor woman on purpose.

Of all days for Delaney to come home, today was the worst possible choice. I was exhausted and anxious about work, and all day, the only thing that had pulled me through was the thought of taking some Nyquil and going straight to bed.

I was just shuffling carrots onto my plate when Delaney decided to grace me with her presence.

She had on jeans and a V-neck shirt, her hair scraped back in a prickly bun. Again, I was drawn to the sharp angles of her face and chest ... and the dark circles under her eyes.

"How was school?"

It was my go-to question these days because there wasn't much else she was willing to share with me.

"Fine."

She sat down, scrunched her nose at the chicken, and dolloped a few scoops of peas and carrots on her plate.

"Is that all you're going to eat?" I asked, putting my fork down and staring.

"I'm trying out being a vegan," she told me, poking one lonely pea with her fork and popping it into her mouth.

"Well, I put butter on those when I cooked them, so I think you've already broken a rule." It came out harsher than I expected it to; I was tired and irritated that there was yet another thing I didn't know about my daughter. Now I couldn't even cook canned peas correctly.

"Sam went vegan, and she lost like, I don't know, twenty pounds."

I scooted my chair back and picked up my plate. Dropping it in the sink, food and all, I whipped back around and looked at Delaney.

"You don't need to lose any more weight, Laney. You're skin and bones already. Frankly, I'm getting concerned."

Delaney narrowed her eyes at me. "You're worried about me? I'm not the one running over little old ladies with my car."

Her words cut like daggers. Clenching my teeth, I watched her storm back to her room. When she was gone, I slumped back down in my chair, massaging my temples.

This is ridiculous. Delaney and I used to be so close and now it's like we're strangers living under the same roof.

Worse than strangers. More like enemies these days.

And sometimes, when I speak to her, I hate the wretched sound of my voice – the nagging mother, the constant critic … but what else can I do?!

I got up and went to her bedroom door. Knocking, I called through the crack, "Come out! We need to talk."

When she didn't respond, I turned the knob. Locked.

I knocked harder. "Open this door now." The seconds ticked by, fury bubbling up inside me. I was still rattled by my behavior at the table the other night, knocking food on the floor like a toddler. I took a deep breath.

I need to approach this, calmly.

"I have nothing to say," came Delaney's soft voice from the other side.

"Well, I do have something to say, and I'm asking you to let me in."

Delaney didn't know I had a key to the door. I didn't want to use it, but it looked like I might have to. Either that or continue allowing her to shut me out of her life permanently.

But then, I heard the click of a lock and the door cracked open.

I pushed on it gently and entered the room.

Delaney plopped down on her bed with a childish huff, then curled her legs up, pretzel-style.

The bed was neatly made, just like it had been the other day. Two math books, a calculator, and Delaney's cell phone lay on the bed beside her and Bob the Elephant. My heart lurched. Seeing her there on the bed … all I could think

169

about was my little girl, waiting anxiously for me to come to her room, to tell her a shadow story ...

I would never admit it, but there were times when I didn't want to. I just wanted her to go to sleep so I could have a little me-time and get to bed early for work. Now, what I wouldn't give to curl up in bed beside her, to tell her a million stories if that was what she wanted ...

I sat down on the bed beside her. She scooted over a few inches, still refusing to look at me.

"What happened with Fran was an accident. I don't understand why you're so angry at me about that. It was an honest mistake. I feel awful about it and I've gone over and helped her out as much as she's allowed me to. You can't really hate me this much, can you? Because it feels like you can't fucking stand me anymore, Laney."

Delaney looked over at me, eyes widening. "I don't think I've ever heard you cuss before, Mom."

"Well, where do you think you get it from? You think you're the only one with anger inside you?" I laughed, but it sounded hollow.

"I know you didn't hit her on purpose," Delaney said, dully.

"Then why are you so pissed off?"

Delaney shrugged. "I guess ... I don't know. Kids at school give me a hard time as it is. And then I have to spend the day defending my mother while they all pass around that stupid article ..."

My stomach ached. "I'm sorry, honey. I hate that they

did that to you. I wish you had said something sooner. I'll call and talk to Principal Gaines in the morning ..."

"No! I don't want you to do that," she said. Then, solemnly, "Please, Mom, don't."

"Okay," I agreed.

I waited for her to say more, but silence filled the room, the sound of it deafening. Finally, I asked, "What else are they teasing you about, Laney?"

I didn't expect her to answer, so when she spoke, I was surprised.

"Because I like boys."

"Okay," I said, softly.

"And I like girls."

"Oh." Words were stuck like peanut butter in my gullet. I tried to think, to come up with the right response ...

"You know it doesn't matter to me who you like, baby. You know that, right?" I said.

Delaney nodded, which was a relief for me.

"I'm really glad you told me. I can't imagine ... it must be confusing for you."

Delaney shook her head harder, flexing her jaw. "Not really. I just like who I like, it's everyone else who thinks it's so weird and confusing."

"Your friends?" I thought about Viola and Kerry.

Were they her friends, or was one of them her girlfriend?

I felt like an asshole for even thinking it. But I wanted to understand what exactly was going on.

As though she could read my mind, Delaney said, "It's

not Kerry or Viola, if that's what you're thinking. They've been ... distant, ever since I told them."

"That was incredibly brave of you."

"Yeah, but now the boys treat me funny, like it's 'hot' that I like girls so they tease me about it. And the girls look at me weirdly, like just because I'm friendly toward them, it means I'm interested in them ... like that, you know?"

"How did they find out?" I asked, tentatively. I was afraid to say anything wrong, afraid of doing something that would halt the conversation completely. It felt good to have her opening up to me but hearing the truth of what she was going through with her peers, made me furious ... and heartbroken.

"Because I'm dating someone."

This is news to me.

"Oh? Is it anyone I know?"

Truth be told, I barely knew anyone in Delaney's life anymore, besides Kerry and Viola.

Delaney shook her head. "Her name is Mary. We met in science lab."

I waited for her to say more.

"Kerry and Viola acted weird about it. Asked me if I 'had a thing for them too'. I told them I didn't and when they asked if I was a lesbian, I tried to explain to them that I was bi. Next thing I know, the whole school is talking ... and ..."

"And?" I reached over and took her hand in mine. For once, she didn't pull away from me.

Delaney reached behind her and picked up her phone. I watched her enter in the same code I'd put in the other day, wordlessly.

She held up the same naked photo of the boy I'd seen the other day. But, wait ... no, it wasn't the same. It was a different photo, but similar. No face, just the lower half, and a boy gripping his penis ... only different, from another angle ...

I felt sick to my stomach.

"Who is sending those pictures?"

"A boy from school. Sometimes he sends messages with them like, 'Come back to the dark side. You can't say no to this dick. Better yet, bring a friend along'."

I cringed, listening to her mimic those hateful, nasty words. "That's so horrible."

"Can I change my number?" she asked, eyes brimming with tears.

"Of course you can. I'll call first thing in the morning and get it done. But about school ... I know you don't want me to say anything, but we have to do something. Will you at least tell me who this boy is? I could call his parents ..."

"Just let me handle it, okay?" Delaney wiped her tears away and sat up straighter, her ego returning.

She flinched when I reached in for a hug, but I pulled her in to me anyway.

"I love you. You are the most amazing girl I know. And you're strong. So freaking strong. We'll get through this, I promise."

And just like that, her body loosened in my arms.

Tears were sliding down my cheeks, but all I could feel inside was my chest boiling over with rage.

I should kill that fucking kid for hurting my daughter.

Startled by the thought, I tried not to think about the last time I'd felt this angry, about how those angry thoughts could easily morph into something darker ...

Chapter 26

1993 - Andrea

It was two o'clock in the morning when my uncle stumbled through the front door. Philomena and I were side by side, squeezed together like two sardines beneath a braided quilt on the couch.

My uncle was off balance, dropping his keys on the floor, then knocking his hip on an end table as he struggled to turn on the lamp and pick them back up.

"What the hell are you still doing up?" He bellowed. He stared at me with that drunken red squint of his, then his eyes darted over to Philomena.

"And who's this? You got a lesbo girlfriend you didn't tell me about me, sweet cheeks?"

I hated that nickname, *sweet cheeks*. My face burned with shame when he said it. I could feel Philomena's hand under the quilt, squeezing mine.

"This is Philomena, a friend from school. I hope it's okay she stayed over ..." I said, clearing my throat.

Uncle Phil let out a loud, long burp and, saying nothing, stumbled on into the kitchen. I nodded at Philomena.

My silent words: *It's time.*

I stood up slowly from the couch, pushing the blankets aside. Philomena stood, too, clutching the cast-iron skillet in her hand in case we had to knock him over the head with it. She'd been gripping it under the cover for hours, trembling non-stop beside me.

"Uncle Phil?" I tiptoed towards the kitchen, where I could hear him shuffling around.

"What?" he belched. I heard the refrigerator bang open, slam back shut, then the pop of a beer can opening.

When he finished chugging his beer, I was standing in the doorway of the kitchen in the dark.

"What is it? Shouldn't you go on to bed now, girl?"

"There's something I need to tell you."

"Well, go on then." He crushed the can in his hands and burped again.

"Two of my other friends came over, too. They're in the bathtub but they won't come out."

"Huh?" he looked at me strangely, one eye open and one eye shut. He was usually drunk when he came home, but tonight, even more so than usual. My guess was that if I let him, he'd pass out in the next few minutes.

"They won't get out of the bathtub," I spoke, louder this time.

"They're in there together?" Phil chuckled. "I knew it! Young girls experimenting, having a little fun ... Well, why don't I check on them for you then, sweet cheeks?"

As he strolled toward the closed bathroom door, Philomena came to stand behind me.

"You ready?" she whispered.

"I think so."

Uncle Phil twisted the knob and opened the door.

"Why y'all taking a bath with the lights off?" He fiddled with the switch, but nothing happened.

"What on God's green earth?" he mumbled.

"The bulb over the sink was loose earlier. It might need tightening. I hope they didn't pass out in the tub ..." I called.

"Stupid asses," he grumbled, stumbling around in the darkened bathroom to get to the sink.

"Now!" Philomena shoved me hard from behind.

I slammed the door to the bathroom shut while she started pushing the cabinet over.

"Hurry!" I shouted, as my uncle shoved on the door. I held the door with all my might, but he managed to get it open a crack. I pressed up against it with all my might pinching his hand in the door in the process.

My uncle howled, a horrible, animalistic sound ...

"Just a couple more inches ..."

Philomena was beat red as she managed to cover the door with the heavy cabinet. I bent down, and together, we pushed it tight against the surface of the door.

"What the fuck is going on!" Phillip bellowed, pounding

the door with both his fists. "This isn't funny, girls! Stop being little bitches, why don't ya?"

"Go call them now. We may only have a few more minutes before he manages to break the door down and escape ..." Philomena warned.

I ran for the phone in the kitchen, praying the cabinet would hold. The phone was yellow with age, the cord so twisted and tangled that I barely had an inch between it and the wall as I dialed.

"9-1-1. What's your emergency?" a woman asked me.

I stared at Philomena and she stared at me as I recited the lines we'd practiced a dozen times over the last two hours.

"This is Andrea Eagon. I live with my uncle, Phil Eagon. I had a few friends over to stay the night. Well, he came home drunk and I think he hurt two of my friends ... We managed to trap him in the bathroom, but I think he's going to hurt us too. Can you please come as fast as you can?"

Chapter 27

NOW

My heart still bucking in my chest, I paced the floor in front of the living-room window, watching for the black truck I'd seen on Grant Street, or any wobbly shadows in the dark.

When her lights appeared, two bulgy yellow cat-eyes at the end of the street, I knew it was her and I released a ragged breath of relief.

I waited for her to pull in and park beside my van. Then I opened the door and waved her inside, hurriedly.

She was rattled; I could see it in her milky brown eyes. Her hair was scraped back in a low ponytail; she was wearing a pair of soft pajama pants.

I closed the door and turned off the porch light, then slid the deadbolt into place.

"What's going on?" she asked, shakily.

Wordlessly, I led her through the living room, past Delaney's empty bedroom, and down the long dark hallway to my room.

I don't know if it was my imagination or not, but the bodies were starting to smell. Something strangely sour, but also sweet, permeated the air.

I opened the door and flipped the light switch on.

As expected, the bodies still lay covered on the floor, side by side. I walked over and stood by the dresser, stiffly.

"Philomena, he's back and he left these bodies for me. For us, I think."

"Why are you calling me that? You're scaring me." Pam reached over and grabbed the meaty part of my upper arm and squeezed.

It's our history, our shared secrets ... that was what had brought her name out of me.

I haven't said it in, what ... twenty ... twenty-five, years? Maybe more than that ...

We had promised to leave it all behind, to leave those God-awful names along with those two dead girls, but old habits are hard to break.

And for a while I was able to pretend none of it had happened, to pretend that we were just us, Ivy and Pam, two best friends from Indiana, two transplants from southern Georgia that were raised by Pam's grandma and ended up in the same stuffy office as co-workers ...

"I'm sorry. It's just ... everything is rushing back to me.

I'm so scared, Pam. He's here. I don't know how he found us, but he did."

"How could he be out of prison already? I thought they gave him a life sentence."

"With parole," I murmured, stepping toward the bodies. I half expected Uncle Phil to spring up from beneath the sheets ...

Calmly, Pam set her purse on my bed, and stepped over to the corpses.

"Who's under those sheets?" she breathed. For a brief moment, I was falling back to that old trailer, to that night we lay tangled under the quilt, clutching that heavy pan as though it could save us from our own evil mistakes ...

She had been calm then, too, but also an edge, always an edge, of fear to her. We had changed, encompassing our new personas, but here we were, just the same.

If I let myself, I could see her for who she was. Without the fake blonde dye and the crinkles around her eyes, she was once again that young, beautiful girl who lit up a room, whose parents were rich and adored her. Who stood beside me, and vice versa ...

We were cut from different cloths, she and I, but somehow, we had understood each other then, as we did now.

I took a deep breath and knelt beside the first body. I pulled the sheet down, far enough so she could see his ashy-white face and the now-black stab wounds in his stomach.

Pam covered her mouth with her hands, horrified.

It's almost like she's never seen a dead body before.

"I woke up to find him beside me in bed. And I have no idea how he got there. I don't remember inviting him over. I don't remember much of anything." When Pam didn't respond, I continued, "He had no license, no shoes ... but there was a car parked out front with the keys inside. A navy-blue Camaro. The registration and insurance were for someone named Robin Regal. The address was on Grant Street, but I don't think it belongs to him because in the bathroom cabinet I found prescriptions for ... Phillip Eagon. And then I heard a car pull up. I know it was him. I ran as far away as I could from Grant Street, then I called an Uber. I don't think he followed me ... but I guarantee he knows where I live. Probably knows where to find you, too," I said, swallowing back a lump in my throat.

Pam was quiet, *too quiet,* so unlike the carefree, bubbly persona she'd adopted since changing her name.

It didn't matter that my uncle was the one accused of the murders, or that he was found guilty when he stood trial. The media had swarmed on my tiny town, and they had pummeled us for interviews and autographs and questions – some of them asked us if we were involved. If it was really *us* that had committed those murders. And Tamara and Mandy's parents never believed our story. They gave interviews with the press, claiming Philomena was a stuck-up rich girl who killed their daughters over a boy.

And, as expected, Uncle Phil didn't go down without

a fight. Sure, he was a mean drunk with a record, but he hadn't killed those girls, and there were witnesses who said they saw him at the tavern that night, that he was happy-go-lucky following news that he'd received a two-dollar raise at the toothpaste factory that day.

He had no motive to kill those girls, not that night. Not ever.

Philomena Nordstrom and Andrea Eagon ... now, they had reasons. One being that Philomena was sleeping with Mandy's boyfriend, and that I was a recluse who got picked on by the girls, and others, at school.

But despite the nasty rumors, Uncle Phil was still found guilty. I told the police about how he had been touching me for years; it was the only part of the story that was true. I told them about the horrible things he often did to me when he was drunk.

Did he deserve to go to prison for life for what he did to me after the tragic death of my parents? I think so. But I'm not so sure a court would agree.

The knife wounds that covered Tamara's body and the suffocation of Mandy ... they weren't the kinds of things that two, young, weak little girls would do. That was something an old, drunken, pervert did.

The jury believed it, and maybe deep down ... so did I. I wanted to forget that night, and for a while, I almost did ...

But Uncle Phil hadn't forgotten. He was out of prison, and I had no doubt he wanted me to pay for what I'd done.

Pam was already tugging on the other sheet.

"Wait. Don't—"

But it was too late.

"Oh my God!" Pam lurched back from the body, nearly stumbling over Robin's corpse. I caught her arm to stop her from falling, but she jerked away angrily, turning around to give me sharp look.

"You did this! I know you did!" She pointed at the other body on the floor, her accusatory eyes burning holes in mine.

She's not the same girl she used to be, I realized.

Truth is, neither am I.

Chapter 28

BEFORE

I arrived at work, still groggy from my stakeout the night before, and took the lift to the fourth floor. No mysterious black trucks had been hanging around outside our house last night ...

I was a few minutes early, and I was relieved to find only Pam in the dimly lit office.

"You're early for once." She was standing near our little break-room counter, watching the coffee trickle slowly down into the pot.

"Yeah."

"What's the matter with you?" Pam clicked her bright red fingernails on the counter, a nervous habit that had driven me crazy for years.

Before I could answer, she added, "I keep waiting for you to tell me more about your dates. I'm assuming you didn't see anyone last night since you're in here so early. You do look tired though." She pointed a finger at what I could only imagine were deep, dark bags under my eyes.

"Forget the dating site. It's Laney. I'm hoping you can help me somehow."

The coffee wasn't done, but Pam moved the pot aside and let the stream fill up a Styrofoam cup instead. "Here." She handed it to me. "Now, tell me what's wrong with our baby girl."

Thankful no one else was in yet, I took a seat in Jerry's leather desk chair and blew steam off the top of my coffee.

It wasn't my place to share Delaney's personal business with anyone, especially about her sexual preferences, but I had to tell Pam something – she was the only one I knew who could help.

"Delaney's getting bullied at school."

Pam shook her packet of sugar so wildly that tiny crystal flakes blew through the air. "What? Who? I'll fucking kill them."

I gave her a knowing look – words like that were nothing to joke about considering our past – but she acted like she didn't even realize she'd said it.

"Who is it? A boy, a girl?"

"Calm down, Auntie Pam. I don't even know who it is yet. It's definitely a boy though, according to Delaney."

"You need to go down there and raise hell."

I shook my head, wincing as I took a sip of the coffee and the steaming liquid burned dozens of taste buds off my tongue. "She doesn't want me to do that. And she won't give me his name. I've got to respect her wishes, but at the same time, I have to do something. I'm her mother. It's my job to fix this shit. Right?"

"Right," Pam nodded, dutifully.

"Does JoAnn in the office still live in your building?"

Although Pam had no children of her own, she was chummy with several of the single teachers and administrators who lived in the same affordable apartment complex near school that she did. I only knew JoAnn Feeler from a few chance encounters, dropping off money for schoolbooks, or picking up Delaney's homework when she was sick. But from what I could gather, JoAnn was the go-to person in the office and she was rather chatty, which meant that if Pam told her what was going on with Delaney, then JoAnn would surely discuss it with the principal and on-staff security personnel.

This would still alert them, without making it look like I was the one who told. But, speaking of their involvement, why hadn't they noticed all this going on?

Perhaps I should pull Delaney out of school and send her somewhere else. Or, what about home school?

It wasn't a terrible option, but ... isn't school just a microcosm for the workplace? Even if I shield her from the awfulness now, she'll still find it later in life, in social circles and her workplace environment ...

"Earth to Ivy ..." Pam snapped her fingers in front of my face.

I took a sip of coffee. "What did you say? Sorry. I'm just worried about Delaney."

"I said I'll go talk to JoAnn right after school. Don't worry. We'll deal with this together. Nobody messes with our girl."

But Pam and I had a shitty way of handling school-age conflict, that was for sure.

Chapter 29

1994 – Andrea

"They're still out there. Those darned vultures," Thomas Nordstrom complained to his wife, Melissa.

Melissa stepped around him, head high and surefooted, and jerked the curtains tightly together in one steady thrust. She turned around and looked to where Philomena and I were sitting, huddled together on a cushy lounge chair in the living room.

"I know it's hard, girls. But now that"—she sniffed and looked away from us—"Andrea's uncle has been charged, it's only a matter of time before he gets sentenced."

"Hopefully to life in prison," Thomas huffed. He was still standing by the window, peeking through the side of the curtains at the dozens of news vans outside.

It was a circus – literally – and we were their favorite clowns. Even the kids at school acted differently around us.

There were two types of people at school, no in-betweens: those who treated us like royalty and those who avoided us like the plague.

After what we did – what we *really* did – I empathized more with those who stayed away.

I would stay from me too, if I knew the truth.

The only good thing that had come out of all of this was Philomena. We had gone through something that no one else could, or ever would, understand. And together, we held the secret that could make or break our futures ...

Thomas and Melissa Nordstrom had shocked everyone, but me the most, when they announced publicly to a local anchor that they would be more than happy to take me in. The media was obsessed with Philomena because of her beauty and charm, and her rich, new family in town to boot, but my story was the one that tugged at all their heartstrings. I'd lost my parents, been abused by my uncle, then lost two of my 'friends' in a horrific double-murder ... and to top it all off, I was now an orphan.

But not according to the Nordstroms.

After that night, when the cops showed up and discovered my raging uncle in the bathroom and the two murdered girls inside, that was the last time I ever stepped foot in that trailer. The Nordstroms handled everything – taking my few meager belongings out after the crime scene had been cleared and bringing them to their house.

My ratty clothes, old books, and worthless knick-knacks didn't quite fit in with the Nordstroms' mansion. There were eight bedrooms in all and half as many bathrooms, and there was a pool and a hot tub ... like something out of a fairy tale.

As much as I enjoyed being there, especially with Philomena, it wasn't as good as I had expected. I still woke up nearly every night, panting and screaming, Mandy's smushed faced beneath that shower curtain and the feel of her body limp in my arms. Those images held me hostage.

Philomena wasn't much better, to be honest. And the taunting at school by our classmates and the harassment by reporters ... it seemed to be getting worse, not better.

I was jumpy, afraid to go outside, afraid that everyone could see through the heart of me, see what I'd done, *really* done.

Melissa was still talking, her voice a distant wah, wah, wah in the background of my muddled thoughts ...

"What do you think, Andrea? I'd like to hear your thoughts on this first ..."

"Huh?" I sat up in my chair, looking around at the three of them.

Thomas, Melissa, Philomena, all three stared at me, waiting for something.

"I'm sorry, I didn't hear you."

Melissa sighed, but then smiled apologetically. "I was saying that you girls can ride it out, ride out this storm. That's what I think you should do. I think that after the sentencing, they'll finally pack up and go. Kids at school will forget; things will eventually return to normal."

"Or?" I pressed, sensing there was an alternative to that terrible option.

"Or," Thomas piped in, "you girls are welcome to go stay with my mother in Indiana. And this is my choice for the two of you ..." Melissa shot him a weary look. I'd heard her mention his mother a time or two over dinner, and I got the impression there was bad blood there.

"Now, it's nowhere near as nice as this place," Thomas warned. "She lives on a small ranch near Madison, Indiana. It's a small town, a small way of life, fewer kids than what you're used to down here. She's willing to take you guys in. She'd old-fashioned, but she's kind ... and it could be a chance to get away for a while. To finish out your last few years of school without all this ruckus going on."

Before I could respond, Philomena said, "But I barely know Grandma Nordstrom! I think I've met her only, what ... once or twice in the past fifteen years? And what happened here, it'll follow us there, just like it follows us here. The kids will find out, and the media too, and then they'll swarm us there instead."

Although the idea had sounded solid at first, Philomena made a good point.

Melissa and Thomas exchanged a look, something secretive between them ...

"I don't want you to go. I'd miss you like crazy. Miss you both," Melissa added, glancing at me, which was kind of her to say but unnecessary.

"But if that's what you want to do, then I think we can

arrange to have your names changed. It may take a few months to do it, but it's very possible. You could get a new hairstyle, some new clothes, and move to Indiana with your new names. Just until this all blows over."

Philomena and I stared at each other, wide-eyed and open-mouthed.

A name change?

It seemed ridiculously absurd, but also kind of cool. I mean, what young girl doesn't occasionally dream of changing her name at an early age?

Memories came flooding back of my mother and I, picking out our unicorn names in one of those silly kids' magazines they sent home from school. She was Star Rose; I was Ivy Raindrop. So silly ... of all the things to remember. But thinking about that day, us rolling on the floor with laughter, calling each other by our new names ...

"Can we choose our names?" I asked softly.

Thomas and Melissa exchanged another glance.

"I don't see why not," Thomas shrugged.

"I want my name to be Ivy," I said, puffing out my chest. I tried to imagine myself as an Ivy, mysterious and beautiful.

Definitely not a killer.

"Okay. What about you, Philomena? Any names you've always dreamed of having?" her mother asked with a wink. Sometimes, seeing them together, the casual day-to-day exchange of a mother and daughter, cut me to the core because I missed my own so much.

In Indiana, we'd be on a level playing field - both orphans

in a way. Although we would be living with her grand-mother, it sounded like she was as much a stranger to Philomena as she would be to me.

"I hate my name," Philomena said, crossing her arms over her chest.

Thomas chuckled. "Well, that's news to us. I always thought you liked it, dear."

"It's too long to pronounce, too hard for people to spell. I mean, look at the papers! Every day someone gets it wrong. I think I want an easy name, something simple and short. Something that nobody will turn their head at, or struggle to say out loud ..."

"What about Pam?" I said, nudging my elbow in her ribs. I was joking, but her eyes instantly lit up and she tilted her head side to side, considering it.

"Pam it is," she said, firmly.

Chapter 30

NOW

"How could you?" Pam looked back and forth between me and the dead boy on the floor. He looked like a child lying there, barely 140 pounds and only slightly taller than my five feet, four inches.

"I didn't," I told her, firmly.

"This boy ... whether he picked on Delaney or not, he has a mother. A sister! What the hell were you thinking?"

If my blood could actually boil, it would have then.

"I. Didn't. Kill. Him!"

But Pam was shaking her head side to side, as though she didn't believe me at all. After all these years, we were practically sisters. I'd never lied to her before.

Why would I start now?

"I found him under the bed. He was like that ... when I found him."

I stared at the sickening wounds on his chest. They looked surreal, like something a makeup artist would do. But he was so pale ... so *dead*.

"Someone must have drugged me. That's all I know. And not *someone*. We know who. Phil. He's back, you have to believe me!"

The room was spinning.

How long has it been since I've eaten?

For the life of me, I couldn't remember eating a thing in the last two days. I felt weak, nauseous. Like I might fall over and pass out any minute ...

"Okay," Pam said solemnly, pulling the sheet back over his body and face.

"Okay?"

"Okay, I believe you. I just don't understand why ... how ... why would Phil kill your daughter's bully and some random stranger, then put them in your room, all while you remained asleep? Something's not adding up here, that's all I'm saying. If he wanted revenge, Ivy, then he'd just come kill us! And you know what we have to do, don't you?"

My mind wandered over to the empty golf bags, then drifted down through the floorboards to the Skilsaw in the basement with the razor-sharp blade ...

"We have to call the police," Pam said.

"Are you crazy?" I shouted. "It'll only be a matter of time before they find out who I really am. Who we both are. You don't think they'll suspect we killed them?"

But as soon as the words were out of my mouth, I realized there was no 'we' this time. The bodies weren't tied to Pam, and they hadn't been found in her house.

Of course she had no problems calling the police – she had nothing to lose this time. She wouldn't lose her only daughter, her house, her freedom ...

"Just go. I'll take care of things on my own," I told her.

Pam reached for me, drawing me in for a hug, just like she had done all those years ago.

As I closed my eyes, I could almost pretend we were fifteen again ... that she was still my best friend, that we would stick together no matter what.

Just me and you, okay?

"I'm sorry, Ivy. But we have to call them. There's simply no other way," she whispered into my ear, still gripping me tightly.

Chapter 31

BEFORE

"His name is Timothy, third of his name ..."

"Come again?"

Pam coughed on the other end of the line. I pulled my ear away until she was done.

"Delaney's bully. I talked to JoAnn just like you asked me to. And apparently she's already solved the mystery."

I felt a wave of relief slide through me.

If they know who he is, then maybe they can do something about it. Put an end to this horrible treatment of my daughter.

"He's captain of the football team, you know the type."

"Not every football player is popular, or a complete ass," I said, sighing.

"Well ... this one is," Pam said. "Hold on."

It was her day at the shelter and in the background, I could hear the lonely mewing of cats.

"So, what did JoAnn say about it?"

Pam coughed again. "Damn cats. My allergies are acting up. Fourteen cats in a small trailer. Can you believe that shit?"

"That's crazy," I said, mutely, waiting for her to get back on track.

"To be honest, JoAnn acted like they already knew. Apparently, this kid has a history of harassing his female classmates ..."

My teeth were grinding involuntarily, the way they always did when I was pissed.

"Let me guess. He's popular, good at sports, and his parents have money."

"You know the McDaniel library they built last year? Well, I'll give you one guess what their last name is."

"McDaniel," I groaned.

I was angry – angry enough to want to burn the whole place down, then dance through the ashes in my daughter's honor.

The nude photo came swarming back, my stomach twisting in knots.

"Well, if they don't put a stop to it, I will."

Pam sneezed into the phone. I waited while she sneezed a dozen more times.

"I got to go. Need to see if there's Benadryl in my locker ..."

"Okay. Thanks for asking her for me. I hope you feel better."

"Ivy, don't do anything stupid. She asked you not to say

anything, remember? Maybe the school will take care of it now that I've said something ..."

"Yeah, maybe," I said, doubtfully.

***

Delaney was staying at her dad's again. He was back from Oklahoma, so I messaged him another reminder about checking the camera footage. He'd promised to message me before he left town last week, but as usual, Michael was a pro when it came to broken promises. He messaged:

I'll do it tonight. Promise.

If I wasn't in such a shitty mood, I would have laughed. Truth be told, I'd probably be better off going around him and asking Samantha to look into it for me.

I strolled through the empty house, picking up stray bits of garbage and clothing, wondering how I'd spend my Friday night. I hadn't logged in to the dating site for days. With everything going on, finding a hook-up had been the farthest thing from my mind.

But the thought of another fun, but brief, encounter with Max made me feel a tiny tremor of excitement. I finished straightening up, then I logged in to my account.

I scrolled through greetings from new members in my inbox, clicked then closed a couple crude photos, then stopped when I saw Ben's name. It had been weeks since our date, and until now, he hadn't called or messaged; he hadn't responded to my string of texts either.

Excited, but nervous, I clicked on the new message from him, noting that he'd sent it two days ago while I was offline.

Ivy,
I just wanted to say I'm sorry for the delayed response.
If I'm being honest, I had a wonderful time with you
the other night. Up until then, I'd been using this site
with only one goal in mind: fun, mindless, one-night
encounters ... But you ... you were something else.
Despite trying to move on from it, I've thought about
you often. Every day, actually. I know you probably
think I'm a complete ass for ghosting you, but I would
like to see you again some time.

I read his message three times, then logged off.
How immature can he be? Does he really think I'm going
to buy his story that I was just so GREAT that he was
intimidated by me?!
I went to the kitchen and opened a bottle of beer. I sipped slowly, my mind circling back to the way Ben had felt beside me, his touch soft but practiced, his lips hurried, but also tender and kind ...
Carrying the beer, I went back to my computer desk and sent a message to him:

What are you doing tonight?
***

201

Three hours and nearly a dozen beers later, Ben and I were tangled like a knot on the couch. Not fucking, but talking, and somehow that felt even more intimate than before ...

"You know it's a crime to send nude photographs of minors, especially if it's nonconsensual," he told me, pointedly.

"Really?" I was in awe of this version of him – he seemed smart, sophisticated, and concerned when I told him about Delaney's bully and the dick pics.

"Really."

"But his face isn't in the photos, so it's a little hard to prove, don't you think?" I pondered.

"You said you saw his number. Do you remember what it was?"

I shook my head. I could remember the area code and first couple digits, but that was it.

"But you pay the cell-phone bill, correct?"

"Yeah ..."

"What provider do you use?" Ben pressed.

When I told him we used Verizon, it only took him a few minutes to set up an account where I could check out my bill online.

"And here, under usage, you can see all the numbers coming and going, for calls, texts, and media messages."

"Really?" I scooted in closer to the screen, pulling up the phone number associated with Delaney's account. I scanned through them, tracing them back to the date I remembered.

"That's it. I'm certain of it." I pointed at the 620 number on the screen. "But how will that help us? Delaney would kill me if I contacted him or his parents."

"But she doesn't know me, and neither does he. Do you trust me?"

In truth, I didn't. I didn't know him well enough for that, but I trusted him more than most people in my life, which said a lot about how isolated I truly was.

I sat on the bed in silence, watching Ben scribble down the number on the top note in a stack of post-its.

"I'll block my number. He won't be able to call back."

"No. You can't!" I said, nipping at nails nervously.

"Don't worry. I know exactly what to say, Ivy."

He looked so sure of himself, so serious. Quietly, I watched as he dialed the number.

Moments later, he grinned at me, then adjusted his mouth into a grim line and said, "Yes, hello! Is this Timothy McDaniel, the third?"

I couldn't hear Timothy's side of the conversation. I closed my eyes, panic rising deep in my chest.

Delaney will kill me if she knows I put him up to this …

"Well, I'm glad you asked. My name is Sergeant Nickels with the Indiana State Police department. How are you doing this evening, Tim? Is it okay if I call you Tim?"

My eyes popped open as I listened in to this one-sided conversation. Not only was Ben pretending to be someone else – a police officer, to boot – but his entire voice and demeanor had changed.

"Me? Oh, I'm not doing too well, Tim. You see, I'm part of the underage-offender tracking team. Your phone number has come to my attention ..."

"Well, yes, ever since the Patriot Act was enacted, we've had the freedom to monitor our citizens' phone calls. Their picture messages, too."

There were several long seconds of silence, then Ben said, "Why have you been sending photos of naked underage boys? Are you aware that is against the law?"

Another pause.

I released a slow breath I hadn't realized I'd been holding.

"Yes, sir, it is. No, I don't care whether they were solicited or not. Or if you're underage yourself. It's still illegal. Now I'm going to have to take down your address, probably come by one day this week to discuss in person—"

Ben set his phone down on the bed between us, then grinned.

"What happened?" I asked, spellbound by his confidence, the quick change in his demeanor.

"He hung up as soon as I asked for his address." His smile widened, and the next thing I knew, we were both rolling on the bed in laughter.

Catching my breath, I rolled onto my left side. He turned on his right, our faces so close we were nose to nose.

"Thanks for doing that. I can't tell you how much it means to me."

"It was my pleasure," he said, leaning in. His kiss was so tender, like the wings of a moth brushing over my lips.

"Do you think it will help?" I asked, eyes still closed from the kiss. As much as I wanted to enjoy this moment with Ben, my heart was still on Delaney. I didn't want to add to her stress or make the boy even more volatile come Monday when she went back to school.

"I hope so," Ben replied. "He sounded like a scared little child on the other end, as soon as I told him I was a cop."

"How'd you do that anyway? Morph into somebody else, just like that?" I rolled onto my back and snapped my fingers, watching his face.

He chuckled. "I don't know. Probably all those years of taking drama classes in junior high." He shrugged.

I guess I'm not the only one who knows how to switch my old self off when I have to.

"Can you help me with one more thing? I still need to change Delaney's phone number. She asked me the other day, and I still haven't done it."

Ben sat up in the bed, looking at my computer. "Sure. That's easy. We just put in a request on the same account we just set up."

"You sure you don't mind?" I asked, sitting up beside him.

"Not at all. It'll only take a second."

While he took care of that, I went to the bathroom and freshened up. My eyeliner and mascara were runny from the laughing and I tried to fix it with a light dusting of cheap concealer. Then I smoothed the stray pieces of hair out of my eyes and gave myself a breath-check in the mirror.

"Who's MaxLove1985?" Ben asked me, as soon as I returned to the bedroom.

I stopped in my tracks, bracing myself. I don't know why; it's not like I owed this man an explanation, or like we were monogamous yet. I guess the real reason for my nerves was Michael. He used to be verbally abusive and possessive at times, so the fear reaction came naturally.

But Ben didn't look angry at all – in fact, he was smiling.

"Who?" I said, swallowing down a lump in my throat.

Ben tossed his head back and laughed. "You're a terrible liar, you know? It's no big deal, Ivy. It's not like we're dating. And I promise, I wasn't snooping. The message came across the bottom of your screen. Something about 'smacking that sexy ass of yours again'."

Embarrassed beyond belief, I reached across him and clicked the off button on my screen.

"When you didn't call or message, I thought I'd try out a few other guys," I said, meekly.

Ben's eyes were pupil-less, his smile deep and delicious.

He wants me. I can tell.

He reached out, taking hold of my waist, and pulled me down onto his lap. In a single motion, I yanked my top and bra over my head, straddling him.

Our kisses weren't as sweet as the earlier ones had been; I dove for him, feverishly biting his lips and enjoying the power I felt over him.

Chapter 32

BEFORE

When I opened my eyes, the sun was streaming through the curtains. Birds were singing their morning song, serenading me back to sleep. My eyes popped open, that usual morning panic setting in.

No, I'm not late for work. It's Saturday, silly, I reminded myself.

I closed my eyes, tugging the covers up to my chin and rolling onto my side. I could smell Ben all over my sheets, the smell of his aftershave, the salt of his skin ...

My hand reached out, feeling the empty, smooth spot beside me.

I knew he wouldn't be there, but still, I'd sort of hoped.

Last night, he'd told me that he had to leave early to help his brother move. He'd set the alarm on his cell phone for 4:30am, but I'd never heard it go off.

I wish he'd woken me up; I would have loved another quick round with him.

I nuzzled my face into the pillow he'd slept on, smiling as I remembered last night – me, loose from the alcohol and empowered by his desire. Making love with him had felt so natural, and so *fun*.

I can't wait to do it again.

I closed my eyes, hoping I could go back to sleep for at least an hour or two.

A knock on the front door gave me a start. For a moment, I considered ignoring it completely. It couldn't be Delaney, because she had a key. Pam or Ben would have called first …

But it might be Fran. She could need help with something, I thought guiltily.

Groaning, I forced myself up out of bed. I was naked, so I tugged on my ratty old nightgown and trudged down the hall and through the living room to the front door.

I could already see her through the opaque windows, that shiny blonde hair and bright blue eyes. The strange ring of a neck brace pushing her chin up.

The living room was a disaster and I looked like a wreck myself, but I sighed and opened the door.

"Hi, Samantha," I said, squinting out at her through the bright morning stream of sun.

"Oh, I hope I didn't wake you," she said, smiling stiffly. She was always stiff, with that perfect posture and those charm-school mannerisms, but she seemed even more owl-like with that brace around her neck.

"I was up, just lying around being lazy. Why don't you come in?"

I opened the door and motioned her over to the living-room sofa.

Slowly and primly, she took a seat on the edge of the couch. I sat down on the opposite end, as far away from her as I could get.

"Is Delaney okay?" I asked.

"Oh, yes. She's great. I left her with the boys. They were watching cartoons together."

I tried to imagine Delaney with a sibling to hang out with. Again, my heart ached for the son I'd lost ...

"And Michael?" The thought of making coffee and offering some to her sprung to mind, but I didn't want her to stay that long.

No, I think I'll just be a rude hostess. Maybe it'll get her to leave sooner.

"Michael left for Reno this morning," she said. She said it so flatly, like she didn't care whether he came or went.

"I thought he just got home from Chicago, or was it Oklahoma?" There was a loose thread on the arm of the couch. I twisted it tight around my ring finger then unfurled it.

"Oklahoma. Yeah, he did. But he had to go again. Well, you know how it is ..."

There were a few seconds of awkward silence between us and suddenly I was wishing I'd never pulled myself out of bed.

209

Unfortunately, I do know how it is.

"What can I do for you?" I asked, getting straight to the point.

Samantha cleared her throat. "Michael went through the camera footage last night and you're right about what you told him. Someone has been hanging around outside our house, too."

I took in a sharp intake of breath.

"You think it's someone watching Delaney?" she asked.

"I do," I said, jaw flexing again. "And I'm pretty sure I know who it is."

The last person I wanted to confide in was my ex-husband's annoyingly pretty wife, but considering she was a major part of Delaney's life now, I decided to tell her the truth.

I filled her in on the McDaniel boy and the harassment Delaney had told me about.

"It was him? The naked pic?"

For the first time, I saw Samantha as Delaney would: her guard down, her shoulders slumped as she covered her face with her hands.

"I want to kill him," she hissed, her words giving me a little shock.

"I don't know for sure it's him who's watching her, but if it is, hopefully he'll be leaving her alone now."

"Why do you think he'll stop?"

I didn't want to tell her about Ben, or the little prank we'd done last night while drunk, but I spilled my secret anyway.

210

I needed to tell someone, and who better than someone who felt as angry as I did about what was happening to my daughter?

"Very clever," Samantha said with a conspiratorial smile. "But," she said, grin fading, "if that doesn't work, I have another idea."

Chapter 33

NOW

There was a dead stranger and a dead classmate of Delaney's in the middle of my bedroom.

It almost felt surreal ... But then again, that old survival mode was kicking in: with or without Pam's help, I had to figure this out without calling the cops. We'd gotten away with murder once ... *but twice?* No, not this time ...

"We can't call them, not yet," I told her, gripping her arms and trying to look her in the face. She was trembling, her face sheet-white, and I regretted calling her in the first place.

"I need to figure this out. I need more time ..."

"When was he released? Shouldn't they have told us or something?" Pam whined.

"How would they have done that?" I snapped. More softly, I said, "we have new identities, remember? Unless they called your parents ..."

Pam's grandmother had been dead for nearly a decade. A kind woman, I'd grown closer to her than Pam had, which I often wondered if she resented. Pam had gone back to Georgia to see her folks a handful of times since we were teens, but I hadn't.

There was nothing left for me back there.

Rarely did I mention our old lives, and just the thought of Pam's parents took me back nearly two decades.

She hadn't mentioned them in years. "Pam, do you still talk to them? I wonder if the cops warned them?"

Pam shook her head. "They would have called and told me, but I haven't talked to them in years. Sometimes I think it's just easier to forget that side of myself, that entire town ..."

This surprised me. I'd always thought – hoped – that she'd kept in touch with the Nordstroms. When they sent us away to Indiana, I don't think they ever expected us to stay away for good. But then again, they didn't know how guilty we truly were.

"It should say somewhere online. If not country-wide news, there should at least be an article about his release in Georgia's local papers ..."

"You're right." Pam straightened up, looking calmer. She did better when she had a task to do. "I'll look it up online. If he's out, we need to know that for sure."

I already knew he was. But what I really needed was Pam's trust and belief in me now.

I needed her on my side, just like I'd needed her decades ago.

As I watched her take a seat in front of my desk, I realized that she'd never sat there before. We'd been friends for so many years, but how many times had she hung out in my room? Were we growing apart after all these years?

Her fingers flew across the keyboard, her back stiff, on a mission like she was when she managed to snag a new sales account at work.

"Anything?" I asked, gnawing on my nail beds. I needed to sit down and breathe, but I was too amped up for that. I paced back and forth, eyes averted from the dead stranger and teen by my feet.

One minute she was typing, and the next, her fingers froze mid-air, hovering over the keys. She shut the computer down and took a deep breath.

"You're right. I-I can't believe it. They let that creep out last month."

"I guess his parole was approved," I mumbled.

"I've read some articles over the years ... he maintained his innocence the whole way through ..." Pam told me, sullenly.

"Depends on what you consider innocent," I scoffed. Closing my eyes, I could still feel the rough patches on his palms, skimming up and down my inner thighs. And his breath – always sour with the smell of stale beer mixed with cheap coffee.

I shuddered.

"You okay?" Pam eyes crinkled with concern.

There she is, my best friend. Does she finally believe me now?

"Fine. So, he's out. What do we do now?"

"It doesn't make sense that he would come here, or how he even found us in the first place."

"Yeah, I know. That's what's confusing me," I admitted.

"He should have stayed in Georgia. You know, a lot of the people there still think we killed those girls—"

"Stop." I squeezed Pam's shoulder, too tight, and she flinched under my fingers. "I can't talk about that night," I said, releasing my talon-like grip.

Pam tried to push the keyboard back into the desk, but it was jammed. Again and again she tried to shove it in evenly.

Pam, even in moments of stress, always the perfectionist, I thought, bitterly.

Chair pushed back, she leaned her face down, eye level with the sliding tray.

"Not now, Pam. Seriously. It's just off-track or something. I probably slammed it in too hard." My focus was back on the dead guys.

How and where can I hide these bodies?

But Pam wasn't listening.

"It's not off-track," she grunted. She was all the way down on the floor now, crawling under the desk and peering up at the tray from the underside. In a matter of minutes, she'd unplugged the keyboard and mouse, then removed the entire tray from the bottom side of my computer.

"There's something down here," she said, fingers tenderly picking at something stuck under my desk.

I groaned. "Pam! Can you get up off the floor? What the fuck is wrong with you, huh?"

My words were awful, laced with anger and fear, but if Pam noticed, she didn't react.

Slowly, she plucked something off the underside and crawled out from under the desk with it in her hand.

"What the hell is that?"

It was a thin wire, like a miniature charging cord. It was gripped in her right hand as she struggled to climb out from under the desk and get back on her feet. I gripped her forearm and helped her up, pointing at the strange wire. "Did you just break my computer?"

Pam panted, "This doesn't belong on any computer. Regardless, it wasn't attached to the modem; it was taped underneath." She handed it to me.

"What for?" I pinched the tiny cord and held it up for a better view. It *did* sort of look like a phone charger. It was thin and white, but instead of a USB on the end, there was an egg-shaped object with holes.

"I can't say for certain, but I'm pretty sure someone's been spying on you."

"Huh?" I tapped the tiny egg thing and examined the shortened cord it was hooked to.

"I think that's a listening device. I only know because I looked into getting one for work," Pam admitted.

"Why in the hell would you do that?"

"Not at the office, at the shelter. You know Randy, my boss? He's always harassing me and the other girls who work there."

"Oh. Gosh, I'm sorry, Pam. Why didn't you tell me?"

Pam shrugged. "Look, I'll show you." Pam leaned over and pulled up the Google search bar. Images of listening devices flooded the screen.

"Well, some of those look like everyday objects," I said, chilled by what I was seeing. There were devices that looked like everyday pens and plugs; there were even a few that came with light domes or switches to make them look like part of the house.

"This looks like an old one. Or one someone made themselves. Who's been in your room?"

"No one." I guarded this place like Fort Knox because it was always a mess.

But that wasn't true anymore, was it?

My mind instantly went to Ben, sitting at my desk only a couple days earlier. I'd even left him alone for a while, while I primped in the bathroom like a complete idiot.

"Oh my God ..."

"What is it?" Pam's eyes were wide with concern.

"This guy I've seen a few times ... Ben. He said he works in computers. And he's been here, twice. He's even been on my computer alone in here. But why ... why would he do that?"

Pam glanced over at the dead bodies. "I'm not sure. But I'm guessing it might have something to do with those guys."

Chapter 34

BEFORE

I didn't expect to hear from Ben. The last time we'd seen each other had gone so well, but so had the time before that, and he'd ghosted me then.

When he didn't message me all day, I wasn't surprised.

I have enough to worry about. And do I really have time for a boyfriend anyway?

"Are you sure you don't want me to wash the towels too?" I was standing in Fran's living room, a laundry basket full of folded shirts and pajama bottoms. She'd been too proud to let me wash her bras or underwear.

Fran shook her head, turning the page in a new book I'd brought her: *Peril at End House* by Agatha Christie. Ashamed to admit I'd never read a Christie novel, I'd assured her it was a good one when she'd asked me what I thought about it.

"Are you sure? I don't want you getting out of the tub and having to drip dry ..."

Fran rolled her eyes. "If anyone should understand my towel situation, it's you. Now that I'm all alone, it takes me a month to go through all the towels. I still have a dozen clean ones in my linen closet."

Is that how Fran sees me, like her, sad and alone?

"Well, I guess I do sort of get it. But you forget that I have a teenager. She needs one towel to dry herself with, a second to wrap her hair in, and a few to mop up the floor with ..."

"She hasn't been home lately, though, has she?" Fran challenged.

There was something refreshing about her blunt personality, but it was grating on my nerves too. She'd never once thanked me for helping, but then again, *I* had run her down with my van.

"Actually, she messaged this afternoon. She's riding the bus here after school." That reminded me, I had very little food in the fridge.

What could I make for dinner tonight?

"I suppose our late-night visitor will be back then, too?"

I shrugged. I was certain that the stalker was Timothy McDaniel, and after Ben's phony phone call and my conversation with Samantha yesterday, I was confident he'd be gone for good from Delaney's life.

"Hopefully not. Want me to put these away for you?"

"No, that'll be alright. I think I'll take a break from you and read my book now if that's okay," Fran said.

"Yes, of course." I tried not to smile as I watched her, eyes jerking rapidly from line to line.

I picked a good one for her, or so it appears …

I let myself out and crossed the deserted street back to my house. It was dark and lonely inside, but not for long. Delaney would be home soon.

I'd left my cell phone on the table when I went to Fran's. Picking it up, I quickly scanned for missed calls, texts, or social media notifications. I had two.

Unfortunately, neither were Ben. The first was a message from Max.

Miss you, hottie. Can I come by tonight?

Rolling my eyes, I clicked on the next one. It was from Rich007:

I'm sorry about how I acted on our first date. I just really didn't want you to go …

Richard. I'd nearly forgotten about that atrocious meet-up and the twenty-dollar mozzarella sticks. I had no plans to contact either of them, but if Ben didn't call soon, maybe I would schedule another fun night with Max …

***

When the bus grinded to a halt out front, I was picking through the cabinets and freezer for a good dinner option.

Maybe we should go out for dinner tonight.

The thought of having a fancy dinner with Delaney was appealing but the truth was, I couldn't afford it right now. With the missed worked days over the last few weeks and the second half of school tuition due next month, I couldn't really afford much besides McDonald's or Wendy's.

The front door creaked open. Excited to see Delaney, I strolled out of the kitchen wearing a smile. It melted when I saw her face.

Her cheeks were red, her eyes flaming.

I know that look. She's furious.

"What happened?" I asked, my thoughts initially leaping to another bullying incident.

But I should have known better: Delaney's rage was almost always directed at me.

Delaney threw her backpack across the living room. It landed with a loud thump next to the stained coffee table.

"What the hell, Laney?"

"You." She pointed an accusatory finger at me. She was so mad, she was shaking.

"What did I do this time?" I groaned.

Her attitude is getting ridiculous, I thought, my own fury mounting.

"I told you not to say anything, and what do you do? You tell the gossipiest bitch in the school office and you get Samantha involved."

"No, I didn't—"

"You did. You and her, you're both the same. Totally unhelpful, and you think you know everything!"

"Who?" I asked, throwing up my hands in defeat.

"You and Samantha. I hate you both. Don't fucking talk to me." Moments later, I heard the slam of her bedroom door and the low sound of alternative music.

Hearing Delaney say she hated her stepmom should have brought me pleasure, but it didn't. I took my phone out and shot Sam a message.

What happened? Delaney is mad at both of us.

Sam's response was instantaneous:

I went down there and talked to Mindy McDaniel, just like I said I would. I told her about what Timothy was doing, about him hanging around our houses late at night, and I warned her that if she didn't address her son's behavior, then Michael and I would pull out our funding for the country club.

Okay. But that still didn't explain how Delaney knew. Had the boy's mom confronted him about his behavior, and instead of stopping, he'd amped up the bullying?
Seconds later, my answer came.

She was horrified when I told her. And she didn't deny that her son might be bullying Delaney. But this is what she told me: Timothy doesn't drive a truck with tinted windows. In fact, he doesn't drive anything at all right now because he's been grounded for weeks. And that's not all. He's been missing for the last two days. The family thinks he ran off and is staying with friends. Apparently, it's not the first time he's taken off after receiving a punishment.

I read through her message a couple times, my mind spinning in confusion. I replied:

If it's not him in the truck, then it's probably one of his friends. He's popular – I'm sure he has little minions that do his dirty work. And it sucks that he ran off, but it doesn't sound too sinister, does it?

Samantha was typing, but then she stopped. For several minutes, the typing reappeared then stopped again.

What is she not telling me?

I was staring at the phone, waiting, when it started ringing. Samantha was calling.

"What's going on?" I answered, breathlessly.

"Delaney didn't tell you?"

I wanted to scream at the phone, but I took a deep breath and said, "Tell me what?"

Samantha lowered her voice a few octaves. "The police were at school today, asking questions. Michael received a call from a Detective Rodriguez. They asked him to come in while they questioned Delaney. According to Michael, they asked her a million questions about the McDaniel boy and the bullying."

"Why?" I asked, gripping the phone until my knuckles turned white. The thought of the police questioning my daughter, Michael there instead of me, infuriated me.

Why didn't he call me?

"Because apparently Timothy hasn't been staying with any of his friends, like his mother thought. It turns out that some of his friends told the cops that Delaney wanted him dead."

Chapter 35

NOW

"It's a set up. I know it is. He's trying to pay me back for what I did."

"What we did," Pam said, softly.

"Only one man has a reason to hate us that much. Phil. But why he did it like this, I'll never understand."

I could feel the pressure mounting, like a boulder on my chest. It had been years since I'd had a full-blown panic attack, but one was on its way; I could feel it.

"Sit down. Breathe. Just breathe." Pam nudged me back onto the bed. I stared at the ceiling, watching the popcorn patterns rise and swirl.

"Where are you going?" I called.

"To get you some water," Pam said, stretching. I watched her go. She closed the door to my bedroom behind her.

I was feeling a little better, my breaths evening out again.

Phil can't get away with this. He can't.

But who put the bug in my bedroom? It had to be Ben. He's the only one who's had access to my computer area. Him and Delaney …

When my phone rang in my pocket, I almost expected it to be him. I stared at Michael's name, my head spinning.

It must be … what, nearly midnight? Why's he calling this late?

And that was when it dawned on me – Delaney might be in trouble.

What if Phil came for her at her dad's house?

"Hello?" My voice sounded scratchy and mean, like I'd just finished screaming. I cleared my throat. "Michael, are you there?"

"It's me," came a small, feminine voice on the other end. *Sam.*

"Sam, what's wrong? Is Delaney okay?"

When she didn't answer right away, I jolted to my feet. "Sam, tell me!" I screamed.

"She's been arrested. Michael followed her to the station." Sam's voice was so tiny and scared, I didn't even recognize it.

"What? Why?"

"They found bloody clothes in the wooded area behind school. They believe they're a match to the boy."

My head turned, eyes examining the dead boy on my floor.

"And?"

"And they also found something else. Delaney's school

226

ID. It was in the grass, only a couple feet away from the body ..."

"That's absurd! Laney had nothing to do with his death!"

Pam was back with the water, eyes wide as saucers. I batted her away as she tried to hand me the drinking glass.

"Well, they don't know for sure he's dead, Ivy ..." Sam said, her voice taking on a strange tone. "It's not like they found a body. But I know she didn't have anything to do with his disappearance. For all we know, he could be alive and well, setting her up because he's obsessed with her ..."

My eyes were glued to his bloody torso and the blue-black knife wounds that matched Robin Regal's.

Timothy McDaniel didn't set up Delaney. And he most certainly isn't alive and well.

My head was buzzing with adrenaline, realization sinking in fast ...

"Michael called an attorney. He's meeting them at the station," Sam said. Then, "Are you still there?"

"Yeah. Why aren't you with them?" I barked.

Sam sounded like she was crying on the other end. "Because someone had to stay behind with the boys. There are more police here, at the house. They have a search warrant. Your house is probably next ..."

Chapter 36

BEFORE

Silently, I moved through the kitchen, warming up a leftover plate of chicken and potatoes, cooking green beans on the stove.

This whole thing was a complete façade; Delaney would refuse to eat dinner – hell, she might not even come out of her room at all – and any appetite I'd had earlier vanished with Samantha's phone call.

Delaney wanted Timothy McDaniel dead, according to his friends.

Well, of course Delaney hated him; she had every reason to. But she certainly didn't want anyone dead, and if the boy *was* missing, it had nothing at all to do with Delaney.

Timothy McDaniel sounded like a delinquent, plain and simple.

But I needed to talk to Delaney. If she knew more, I

needed her to confide in me. But the last time she'd confided in me, I'd broken her trust ...

"Delaney, dinner's ready," I called through the door.

Ten minutes later, she plopped down at the table with a loud bang.

Quietly, I took a seat across from her, watching in horror as Delaney started wildly shoveling food into her mouth.

Her cheeks were full of chicken and potatoes and when she saw the disgusted look on my face, she smiled at me with her mouth full of food.

"Delaney!"

"What, Mom? I don't want you calling me too skinny! Is this better?"

I sighed deeply.

These stupid games have to end.

"I know you're pissed off at me. But you're not a child anymore, Delaney. You can't act like this. I'm your mother and I need you to talk to me."

"Like I did the other day?"

"I didn't go to the school secretary. She's Pam's neighbor, so Pam asked her a few questions ..."

"So, you ran and told Pam then? How is that better?" Delaney said.

I shrugged, unsure what to say anymore.

"I only want what's best for you, honey. I would never try to hurt you or make things worse for you. Samantha told me that the police came to school. Did they ask you a lot of questions?" I picked up my fork and used it to squash one of the small potatoes flat.

"I know you do. But I'm still mad. Yeah, their questions were stupid. They wanted to know if I knew where he was. If I had anything to do with him running away." Delaney spit a mouthful of food into her napkin and stood up.

"Do you know where he might have gone?" I asked, tentatively.

"I don't know where that asshole went. And frankly, I don't care. If something bad happened to him, then he probably deserved it." Her bedroom door clicked shut and I sat at the kitchen table, numbly picking at my food.

Chapter 37

NOW

"They're coming!" Frantically, I ran from the room and charged down the basement stairs, nearly twisting my ankle in the process.

"Who?" Pam shouted from the top of the stairs.

"The police! They've arrested Delaney. They found Timothy's clothes and her ID behind the school. Don't you see, he's not trying to frame us for the murders, Pam! He's trying to hit me where it really hurts – my daughter!"

"But why would he care about hurting Delaney?" Pam bent her head side to side, considering my theory. I pushed her aside as I reached the top of the stairs, Skilsaw in hand.

"Are you crazy?" Pam shouted, following me back to my bedroom. "You can't do this! You can't!"

"I have to move these bodies somehow. I can't let my daughter go down for a murder she didn't commit, all because of something I did – *we* did – when we were young."

I pressed the sharp side of the saw to Robin Regal's neck, trying to force myself to turn it on. My stomach heaved and the blade shook. I dropped it, running for the commode.

I didn't make it in time. Vomit sprang from my mouth and nose. Huddled by the toilet, I couldn't help thinking about Tamara twenty years earlier …

I wiped my mouth and laid a towel down over my mess, then quickly splashed my face with cool water in the sink.

When I returned to my bedroom, Pam was gone.

Did she take off and leave me? Did she decide that the best thing for her own safety was to cut and run?

But then I heard a thump in Delaney's bedroom.

"Pam?"

The door to Delaney's room was halfway open, light shining through it. I pushed it open.

Pam was opening and closing drawers.

"What the hell are you doing?"

"Just checking," Pam said, looking up at me guiltily.

"Checking for what exactly?"

But I already knew. Pam doesn't believe me about Uncle Phil. She thinks Delaney might be guilty.

"She wouldn't hurt anyone. She's not like me, Pam … and if you're not going to help me, at least get the fuck out of my house so I can do what needs to be done."

Pam lifted Delaney's bed, peeking between the mattress and box springs.

"There." She pressed her hip against the mattress, propping it up as she pointed at something lying flat in between.

"It's a knife," Pam said, giving me a knowing look.

But I wasn't looking at where she was pointing. My eyes were drawn to something else on the floor. A fleck of shiny gold wrapper peeking out from under the bed. I got down on my knees and retrieved the candy wrapper.

"Wait a second ..."

I ran for the kitchen, instantly throwing back the lid on the garbage. I dug through the putrid sack, tossing potatoes and soda cans, and rolled up balls of tissue, into a pile on the floor.

"Now that's what I'm looking for," I breathed. At the bottom of the trash bag was a gold box, wrapped with a big gold ribbon. I reached for it, brushing slimy green beans and crud off the top of it.

When I opened it, it was empty, just as I knew it would be.

The date with Ben. The box of candy ...

The events of last night suddenly rushed back like a tidal wave, too heavy and powerful to stop them ...

Chapter 38

BEFORE

I tried watching TV, anything to get my mind off Delaney and the missing boy, but every local station was talking about the "brilliant young boy" gone missing. The news called him a hometown hero, a rising star, a pillar of the community ...

It made me sick to hear it.

Timothy McDaniel was a bully. Why don't they mention that?

But at the same time, I felt terrible for his mother. Bully or not, I knew how difficult raising a teen could be. His mother and father were probably sick with worry, but I was worried about something else: his disappearance making things even worse for Delaney. The last thing she needed was more strange looks, more isolation ...

I flipped the TV off and went to her bedroom. The door was still closed, the lights out. When I turned the knob, I was surprised to find it unlocked. Delaney was curled up on her side in the dark, purring like a kitten.

My sweet little girl.

She's not so little anymore, and most days she isn't sweet either.

I fought the urge to lie down beside her. Finally, I closed her door and sauntered into the kitchen. I poured myself a glass of cherry Moscato, closing my eyes with joy as I took the first fizzy swallow.

I carried my drink to my bedroom and closed the door, then flicked my computer screen on.

Had it been a waste of time, joining the dating site?

Not really. It was fun, but hard to make real connections online. So many people just wanted to hook up. And even the good ones, like Ben, seemed kind of shady.

Once again, he hadn't called or messaged.

But who cares at this point? I have enough on my plate to worry about already, I decided.

I drained the rest of the wine as I deleted messages from Richard, Max, and a few newcomers. I wasn't in the mood for any of them.

Nevertheless, I found myself back on Ben's profile page. One glass of wine wasn't enough to get me drunk, but I could feel the tightness in my chest loosening ... and again, the urge to send him a message was strong.

Before I could change my mind, I wrote:

Hey you. I'm pretty hurt you still haven't called. I don't understand. You're great in person, but then you disappear ... I just don't think I can see you anymore.

I tipped my wine glass up, letting the last few drops linger on my tongue. I considered getting another glass, but it was already 9:30. Delaney had gone to bed early

Maybe she has the right idea.

I was just digging out my nightgown for bed, when my phone beeped. Ben.

Are you free? Want to meet for a quick coffee at the Waffle House by you? I can explain my behavior.
Explain his behavior? That doesn't sound good.

I looked back and forth between my cozy old nightgown and my phone. Waffle House was only a few miles away, and Delaney was sleeping. Even if she wasn't, Delaney was old enough to be home alone.

In the kitchen, I scribbled a hasty note:

Ran out for milk.
Be back in a half an hour.
– Mom.

I locked the front door behind me and flipped the porch light on, backing out of the driveway ...

Chapter 39

BEFORE

"I'm married."

I wish I could have said that his words were a huge surprise, but by the time I arrived at Waffle House, they were already on the back of my own tongue.

"Big surprise," I'd told him, adding two packs of Sweet 'n' Low to my coffee and swishing it in a slow circle.

I left my daughter home alone for this. What a waste.

"But I'm getting ready to file for divorce. Being with you has really opened my eyes. I deserve to be happy, Ivy."

I nodded, sipping the coffee in silence.

"Do you still want to see me?"

Did I still want to see him? Of course I did.

"I can't. I'm sorry. If you do get divorced, call me once the dust settles, but not before," I said sadly.

I stood up and took one more long drink of coffee, then dropped a five down on the counter.

"Nice knowing you, Ben."

***

Thirty minutes later, I was pulling back into my graveyard-like subdivision. Part of me wanted to cry or scream, but then again, I had too many other things to cry over.

Ben is just one guy. Like the site says, there are plenty of fish out there. They may or may not be found on dating sites ... but they're out there. Somewhere ...

As I pulled into the driveway, my skin crawled. Something felt different, *off*, about the house ...

I put the van in park and looked around. The night air was silent and still; no suspicious vehicles, no strangers looming in the dark ...

Fran's house was dark, but for one light. A lamp was on in her bedroom.

She's probably reading that book, I thought, holding back a small smile.

Fran was grumpy and blunt, but I'd grown to like her. She was like the nagging mom I never had ...

I locked the van and walked toward the house, keys in hand. That was when I realized what was different: the porch light was off.

I could have sworn I flipped it on, on my way out the door ...

As I unlocked the door, my body was on high alert.

What if someone is inside? What if that boy is here, come to hurt Delaney?

I entered the living room, quietly locking the door behind me, then tiptoed through the dark living room.

"Mom."

I let out a startled yelp as Delaney sat up on the couch in the dark.

I stumbled around, reaching for the switch to the lamp. Delaney looked half-asleep, her eyes squinty.

"Where have you been?" she asked.

There was Vitamin Water and a package of Cheez-Its on the floor.

"Didn't you get my note? I went out for milk." But as soon as the words were out of my mouth, I realized how idiotic they truly were.

"So then where's the milk?" Delaney asked.

"They were out of milk," I lied.

I'm tired. So tired. And the last thing I want to do is stand here answering questions about a man I'm never going to see again.

"What are you doing up? You were asleep when I left. I hope the front door closing didn't wake you up?"

Delaney shook her head and stood up stretching.

"I'm going back to bed. I'm so sleepy for some reason. And no, you didn't wake me up. The doorbell did."

"The doorbell?"

Delaney was already headed back to her room, dragging her feet like a zombie.

"Chocolates. They were on the front porch. I hope you don't care but I ate a bunch of them." She thrust a shiny gold box at me, then closed her door. I heard the lock clicking from the other side.

I stared down at the box, confused. Through the door, I said, "Delaney, it's not smart to eat sweets from someone you don't know. I thought I taught you that when you were five ..."

"They're from Sam," she said, I could already hear the sleep in her voice. She'd be asleep within seconds, probably purring like a baby again.

I opened the box of chocolates and selected several for myself. Delaney was right; she had eaten a lot of them. More than half.

Stupid Samantha. Always has to be mother of the year. She probably felt guilty for confronting Timothy's mom and these are her way of apologizing to Delaney ...

The chocolates were softening, melting in my hand. I threw the empty box in the trash, then headed to bed, munching on the milky chocolates along the way ...

Chapter 40

NOW

"They're from Sam." I stared at the empty box of chocolates, the mystery gift that had been delivered while I'd snuck out to meet Ben ...

"What did you say?" Pam came over to me and took the box from my hands. She turned it over and back, then gave me a perplexed look.

"Someone left these on the front porch. Delaney said they were from Sam, but she was so sleepy. I barely heard her through the door; she ate some, and I did too. Next thing I know, I'm waking up in bed with a body beside me, and another one under my bed. We were drugged."

"You think it was Ben who left the candy? Or one of the other guys you've been dating? Sam wouldn't try to drug her own stepdaughter, would she?"

Pam went over to the kitchen window and looked out.

She turned around in front of the sink and pressed her backside against the counter.

"This is fucked up, Ivy. We have to let the cops sort it out this time. There's no other way."

I was still holding the empty box in my hands. I clutched it to my chest. "I can't do that, Pam. I'm sorry, but there's no way I'm letting Delaney go to jail. The bodies in our house, the knife in her room. I know she didn't do this. It's that bastard Phil, trying to frame my daughter for murder, just like I framed him all those years ago. Why is that so hard for you to believe?"

"If that's the truth, then the cops will figure it out. They'll go to that apartment and arrest Phil. They'll listen to your story; I know they will."

"You're free to leave. I won't tell the cops who you really are, or that you ever came here tonight. Just please let me figure out how to hide these bodies until the search is through and I have a little more time to think," I pleaded.

I didn't wait for her answer. I trudged back to the bedroom, determined to squeeze the bodies into those bags this time ...

"Stop." I felt something hard press down between my shoulder blades. Then I heard an eerie click.

Pam just flipped the safety off. She has a gun ...

I took a chance, slowly turning to face her. If I could just see her, just look into my friend's face, maybe I could reason with her.

But she had that look in her eyes – the pure steel of

determination. I'd seen it a thousand times: when she was determined to close a sale, when someone had pissed her off ... and that night in the bathroom right before the showdown with Mandy and Tamara ...

"They're from Sam," I said the words loudly and slowly. I thought about that day in the driveway, watching my only daughter pull away with her dad.

I taught you how to tie your shoes.

But that wasn't what she thought she heard ...

"She was pissed off at Sam. And when she's angry she doesn't call her Sam, she calls her Samantha. What she said that night was 'They're from Pam'. Isn't that, right?"

Pam gave a slight shrug.

"You drugged us. Why? So, you could bring those bodies inside? Try to frame me for murder? Why would you do that?"

Despite the hard mask, Pam's hands were shaking. She still didn't lower the gun.

"Look, it's not how I wanted to do things. But I couldn't let her have the money."

Money. This is about money?!

"You know as well as I do that I don't have any money." I begged.

"Yet," Pam said, bitterly. "Well, not you, exactly. But Delaney was about to get a windfall when she turns eighteen. You never even realized, did you? That Granny was rich. She's the reason Mom and Dad had so much and lived the way they did. She's the one who bought my father his company. She squirreled it all away, living modestly in that shitty little house in the middle of nowhere. And when she died, I just assumed she'd leave it all to Mom and Dad and they'd give it to me. But no, of course not, Granny could never just make things simple ..."

"What are you talking about?"

Pam's grandmother had been dead for nearly a decade. I hadn't heard a word about any money ... not while we were staying there, and not after she died.

"She didn't leave her money to Mom and Dad, or to me. Instead, she left a trust for both of us, for you and for me. But here's the kicker. It's not for us, per se, but for our children. 'Children are the future', she used to say."

I did remember hearing her say that several times. She was an old-fashioned lady who often encouraged both Pam and me to be on the lookout for a good husband, good father material.

"Why would she leave it to our children? I don't understand. I wasn't her blood."

"Because she adored you and she wanted to make sure that our children wouldn't struggle when it came time to go to college. And she didn't want us struggling to send them off into the world."

"Okay ..."

The Skilsaw is on the other side of the room. If I ran for it, could I grab it in time?

"Who was in the black truck, then? You?" I asked, incredulously.

Pam snorted. "I thought if I pressured Delaney into thinking she was being stalked by that stupid boy, she might tell you sooner. I needed it to be convincing. A clear motive. But that girl is stubborn. Then, when you came to me and told me about the bullying, it was like handing me Delaney on a silver platter. I told all the ladies in the office and the principal, too. I wanted the whole town to know Delaney had a reason to kill him."

Clenching my teeth so hard together they threatened to crack, I asked, "Where did you get the truck?"

"It's Jerry's. His mom left it to him when she died, but he never drives it. If you paid attention to your friends, anyone other than your precious little self and your bratty daughter, you already would have known that," Pam snapped, arrogantly.

"Does Jerry know what you're doing?"

For the first time, I saw a flicker of guilt on her face. "No, Jerry's a good guy. He's not interested in dating, but I think I'll talk him into it when I'm filthy rich. We can both quit that shithole job and go somewhere new to start our life together."

I sighed. "Pam, I'm sure Delaney would have shared the money. Do you really think we're that selfish? We have always considered you family."

"One can never be too certain, and she's turned into quite a little bitch these days."

I flinched at the word, my fury rising ...

"And I can never have children. I went to the doctor several

245

years ago, and he told me I was sterile. So, it's not like I would have benefited at all from the money. It wasn't fair for my family's money to go to some trailer-park trash like you. We took you in and helped you out ... and then my stupid grandma snubs my mom by leaving everything to the children of the future. She knew damn well I didn't want kids."

"I'm sorry." Strangely, I did feel sorry.

When had Pam become this sad, manipulative, evil person? Or had she always been this way and I was just blind to it?

"Don't be. All that money will be mine. The will stipulated that our children would receive it when they turned eighteen, granted they're not in prison or incapacitated."

The hairs on my arms stood up. So, this is why. She does want to frame my daughter.

There was no way out of this room but through – and Pam was standing in the doorway, gun aimed straight for my heart.

I'm going to have to take a chance and rush at her, or either run back, or get that saw ...

"How is Phil involved? Has he been helping you?" my voice quivered.

Pam threw her head back and laughed, startling me. For the first time in a long time, she had become completely unrecognizable to me.

"No. Phil is in prison, just as he should be. Just as he *always* will be."

"No, that's not true. I saw his name on those prescription bottles ..."

"Just like I knew you would," Pam said haughtily. "Your prints are all over Robin Regal's apartment. I didn't plan to kill him, at first, just the boy. But it helps that your prints are there as a back-up plan. Maybe the cops will think you helped Delaney with the murders."

Before I could even ask, she went on: "We were dating for a while, me and Robin. I met him on that same stupid site you were on. I told him about my plan, offered to cut him in if he agreed to help me. Moving bodies is a tough business, let me tell you! But then that asshole went and got greedy. I should have known better, honestly. He threatened to go to the cops and tell him who I was and what I planned to do, if I didn't give him ten thousand dollars within twenty-four hours. You and I both know that wasn't an option. He helped me bring in the boy and then he became my next victim. Stupid prick. You slept through it all, like a little baby." Pam giggled, as though we were talking about something as nonchalant as work-place gossip.

I took a couple steps back, pretending I was off-balance. *The closer I can get to the saw the better …*

"I used our printer at work to make the labels. If you'd been a little smarter, you would have realized they were fakes. I just covered up Robin's labels with fake ones for Phillip Eagon."

"But why? Why make me think Uncle Phil was out of prison?"

"Just having a little fun, I guess. Just like I did with the listening device I found on your computer. I had it in my pocket the whole time. Brought it with me!" she laughed harder, giggling through her nose like she used to when she was young. I used to find it endearing, but now I saw it for what it really was: sinister.

Philomena Nordstrom was a sociopath and always had been.

"And I needed to make sure you didn't go to the cops. If you knew your identity was on the line and Phil was back, I was confident you wouldn't do that. I wanted them to link Delaney to the crime all on their own, which brings me to that stupid boy. I paid him to pick on Delaney, not in money but favors, if you know what I mean ..."

I tasted bile in the back of my throat. "Urgh."

For the first time, I actually thought about how it might feel to carve up Pam's face with that saw ...

I think it'd feel pretty good now I know she orchestrated my daughter's bullying and murdered two people, including another child she manipulated into doing her bidding ...

"He didn't even see it coming. I had him meet me out in the woods behind the school. It never even dawned on him that I was wearing gloves. You should have seen the look on his face when I stabbed him. I have to be honest, Ivy, killing again felt good. Like doling out my own kind of justice. Nobody will miss that preppy prick, or that slimy bastard, Robin. Just like nobody misses Tamara and Mandy. I know you know what I mean ..."

She thinks we're the same. She thinks I actually enjoyed killing Mandy. She can't really believe that. I'm not like her, am I?

But I thought about the lifetime of lies. Would I be proud if Delaney knew the truth about me? No, I wouldn't.

I stared down the barrel of the gun. If I died today, then it would be well deserved.

But I can't do that. If I let her kill me, what would happen to Delaney?

"If you kill me, the cops will know it wasn't Delaney. You can't just group me in with the other bodies. Delaney's in custody right now. And I talked to Samantha on the phone, remember? There's a time stamp for everything ... they'll never buy it. It'll fuck up your whole stupid plan," I snarled.

"Bingo! And that's why you have to kill yourself. Well, not actually, but I'm going to make it look that way. After all, it's your gun. And after you got word of your daughter, you sent me a text message. That you knew she was a killer and you couldn't live with yourself anymore."

"No, I didn't," I whispered, horror rising. I already knew what was coming next.

"I sent it from your phone to mine while you were scrounging around in the basement, freaking out over Phantom Phil. And I took your gun. I mean, seriously, Ivy? You're still using the same password for everything, including your gun safe? How fucking stupid can you be?"

Pretty fucking stupid apparently. Stupid for letting her

talk me into the murders all those years ago. Stupid for trusting her ever since …

If I don't do something quick, she's going to kill me. How much longer can I keep her talking?

I took another chance and stepped backward. The saw was just a few feet away …

"Don't move." I froze, not because it was Pam's warning, but another voice entirely.

Pam slowly turned around, looking at someone behind her in the hallway.

"Drop the gun." I recognized that irritated voice. *Fran.*

"No fucking chance, Granny." Pam raised the gun.

There was a blast, the loudest noise I'd ever heard and, as though in slow motion, I watched Pam's body fly and land with a thump by the bed.

Blood seeped out of a baseball sized wound.

Fran stepped through the doorway. She was holding a 12-gauge shot gun, smoke trickling from the end of the barrel.

"Oh my God, Fran!"

She dropped the gun and fell to her knees, clutching her arm in pain. Her cast was partially off.

"Oh, Fran." She had obviously removed it herself in a hurry; I could see where she'd snipped the plaster off with snips, or some other tool.

"How did you know?" I asked.

"I came to return that book and I heard talking. I just had a bad feeling. I have an instinct for these kinds of things. Now quit asking stupid questions and go make sure that psycho is dead. You don't read enough books, do ya? They always pop up and try to go another round."

Just to appease her, I went over and knelt on the floor by my friend.

She's not your friend, Ivy. She never really was …

But seeing Pam there, blood seeping out from her mid-section like a wild river, eyes wide, mouth twisted in a painful O, I felt myself mourning her.

I mourned for the friend I thought she was, the friend and sister I'd always wanted, but never had.

"She's dead, Fran," I said, dully.

Fran was gritting her teeth, holding her injured arm tight to her side with her left arm.

"I'll call an ambulance," I said, taking out my phone.

When I looked back at Fran, her face was sheet white. She was staring at the bodies on the floor.

"Oh. I'll explain those later," I said, holding the phone to my ear.

***

When the police arrived, they took one long look at the three dead bodies and the injured old lady and they slammed me to the ground and cuffed me.

It was the best feeling in the world.

I was alive. Delaney was innocent. And there would never again be a reason to lie.

251

As the cops pulled into the station, sirens blaring, we were met with a crowd of reporters. For the first time in my life, I was glad to see them.

As they led me out of the police car and into the station, I was hammered with flashing lights and manic questions ...

I don't think they expected me to give a comment, but I looked straight into the first camera lens I saw, and said, "My name is Andrea Eagon. You may have heard that name before ..."

Epilogue

1 year later

The prison doors clicked shut behind me, a welcoming sound I hoped never to hear again. As I stepped outside, my eyes burned, not used to the bright white sun and the chilly wind in my face.

It was October when they locked me up. Now it's October again.

Almost like I didn't miss a thing.

But, deep down, I knew that wasn't true.

"Mom!" Delaney was running, dark hair flying behind her like the most gorgeous kite I'd ever seen. She fell into my arms, her full weight bearing down on me. I held on, staying strong and holding onto my baby, the way a mother must always do.

"Mom ..." Delaney said again, tears in her eyes. Suddenly, she straightened up, fixing her hair, adjusting her demeanor as she realized there were reporters flashing pictures nearby.

Some things change, and some never do, I thought, cheerily.

"I missed you, too," I told her.

369 days I'd spent in prison. It seemed pretty brief considering all that I'd done.

Since I was a child at the time of the murders, and under the influence of a "crazed killer", the court had been lenient on me. As far as they were concerned, the true killer was dead and buried.

It was still hard for me to think of Pam as a "crazed killer", but that was exactly what she'd turned out to be. With Fran as a witness and a trail of lies and evidence to prove Pam's guilt, it was pretty easy for them to figure out that I was solely a decoy in the murder of Timothy and Robin.

Time served plus two years of probation.

And the timing was perfect because in two years, Delaney would be the recipient of five million dollars.

We'd already discussed her plans – they were small and reasonable. She always had been smarter than me. She wanted to use the money to pay for art school and she wanted to buy a place far from Indiana, for the two of us. But for the next two years, we were stuck here because of my probation. But I didn't mind it.

Anything beats prison. And everything beats being dead.

"Sam's in the car, waiting," Delaney told me. I noticed she had put on weight. She looked healthier and happier than when I'd last seen her.

Being away from her had nearly killed me, but I knew that her dad and Sam were taking good care of her.

"And your dad? Did he come, too?" I asked, letting Delaney lead me to Sam's car in the lot.

"No. You know how he is. But he'll get over it."

I did know. Michael had been unsupportive and angry, as I had expected he would be. If it was completely up to him, I think he would have tried to stop Delaney from ever seeing me again. But, according to Delaney's letters, Sam had defended me in my absence. She had insisted that all girls need their mothers, and that the best thing would be to let Delaney choose for herself.

Delaney hadn't told Michael about her plans to leave town when she turned eighteen and received her inheritance, but we'd cross that bridge when we came to it ...

"Hi, Sam." I smiled at my ex's wife. She was sitting in the passenger's seat of her Beemer, hair perfectly straightened and makeup flawless.

"You look lovely," I told her.

"You look ... happy to be out," she said stiffly.

"Please tell me I'm not driving." I pointed at the empty driver's chair.

"Nope. I am." Delaney wiggled her eyebrows at me.

"Oh, hell ..."

Braxton and Brock were in the backseat. I climbed in

between them, pinching each of their cheeks. Like Delaney, they had grown too.

I buckled my seatbelt tight as Delaney lurched forward in the prison parking lot. I wasn't ready for a teenager with her license, but I guess we're never fully prepared for what life throws our way. I strapped myself in and hoped for the best.

"Where are we headed?" I asked, watching trees swirl by as Delaney merged onto the highway. It felt strange being out, but also strangely normal.

I heard through the grapevine that Uncle Phil had been released. As far as I knew, he wasn't planning to come find me ... but only time will tell. I'm just glad he was punished for a while for the things he did to me, even if they weren't the things they locked him away for in the first place. I also heard that Jerry quit and moved back home to Alabama. He always had been closer with Pam than me; I guess he probably couldn't face me coming back.

"Oak Hill," Sam said, glancing back at me with a smile.

"Our old neighborhood?" I asked in horror. My future was so uncertain: no job, nowhere to live, two long years of probation. But one thing was certain: I couldn't afford to rent or buy one of those ghost houses in Oak Hill.

"Michael and I bought a house for you both there. Once you get a job and get back on your feet, you can pay us rent."

"Oh." I was shocked; I didn't know what to say.

"I told Michael that it's an investment because, honestly,

it is. Several families have recently bought homes there and they've finally started construction on the pool," Sam added.

"Oh?" This was shocking news to me. "Why would people be moving there all of a sudden?" I asked, perplexed.

"'Cause it's Oak Kill," Brock squawked. Then his brother started laughing.

"Oak Hill," I corrected him, pinching his nose.

"No, he's right, Mom. People are calling it Oak Kill since what happened there. I guess it's quite the popular place all of a sudden. I even heard that people are planning to trick-or-treat in our neighborhood this year."

"Oh, joy," I said, dully.

As Delaney followed the familiar roads, I could almost pretend that nothing had changed, that we were just going home, living our lives, the way we always did.

Delaney pulled into the neighborhood. For a moment, I thought she was going to our old house, but then she pulled into the house beside Fran's and parked.

I laughed, heartily. "Are you telling me you bought the house right next to Fran's? Oh, I bet she loves that."

"She missed you, too," Delaney said, tearful eyes catching mine in the rearview mirror.

I'll believe that when I see it, I thought, drearily.

Fran was standing in the driveway, hands on her hips, when we got out.

Her arm was no longer in a cast, and despite the botched healing process, it looked just fine.

I was about to wave hello, when Fran's front door opened and a handsome man with reddish-brown hair and soft green eyes came waltzing out. He stopped mid-stride when he saw us.

"Wow. Fran's boyfriend is rather young," I whispered to Delaney. She giggled.

"That's her son, Mom. You're really demented, you know that?" She smacked me in the chest with her hand.

"Long time no see. How was the slammer?" Fran asked, crossing the short patch of grass between our driveways. "I'd give you a hug, but I don't do hugs."

"That's alright, Fran. How are you?"

"Oh, you know, old as fuck and grumpy as hell. The usual. This here's my son, Charlie. You two are the same age, practically babies."

Charlie stepped over and stuck out his hand. I shook it, impressed with the strength of his grip. Unlike his mother, Charlie seemed to have some manners.

"After what happened last year, she finally let me come help her," Charlie said, talking out the side of his mouth.

"I heard that! Is that what you call it? Helping? I call it harassment," Fran snapped. "Now, be a doll, and go fetch that pie," she waved him away.

Brock and Braxton latched onto one each of Sam's legs. Delaney and I giggled, watching her stumble around the yard like Frankenstein trying to shoo them off.

Ah, the joys of young motherhood. I'll miss some of parts of it, but not all.

Moments later, Charlie was back, carrying a sweet-smelling blackberry pie.

"Thought I'd return the favor. The only difference is my pies are actually edible," Fran barked.

"Thank you, Fran. Would you both like to come over and share this with us? We have a lot of catching up to do."

"No," Fran said. At the same time, Charlie said, "Yes."

He tugged his mother's arm, and they followed us into the house. Charlie set the pie down in the kitchen and I couldn't help noticing he wasn't wearing a wedding ring.

I'd expected the house to be bare, but there was already some furniture inside. A small dinette table, and a few modest living-room and bedroom furnishings. It was the twin of our old house, but a better, fresher version.

"Thank you again, Sam. There's no way I'll ever be able to thank you enough."

"Well, don't thank me too fast. I have something to tell you later," Sam said, under her breath.

"Listen, Sam. My nerves are kind of shot and I've had enough secrets to last me a lifetime. Can we just skip the anticipation and get on with what you need to say?"

Sam took a deep breath. "I left Michael. Well, more like he left me. Apparently, he met someone while he was out of town on business ..."

"Oh God. I'm sorry." Truly, I was. No one deserved to put up with that asshole, including her.

"Don't be. It's for the best. Now that Delaney has her license, she can come visit me and her brothers whenever she likes. And Michael got his own apartment. I have a feeling that Delaney will be spending most of her days with you now."

She reached in and hugged me so tight I could barely breathe.

Then she dashed off before I could say more, chasing Brock and Braxton through the house.

In the kitchen, I helped Charlie and Fran serve the pie. Fran was right: she's a hell of a baker.

Delaney was setting plates on our new table and when she looked up and saw me smiling, she half-smiled back at me. One good thing about prison: it gives you a lot of time to think. I thought about Dillan every day. But mostly, I thought about my lovely Delaney, and how, inside of her somewhere, she carries part of my son – her brother – with her every day. In an odd way, I have them both. They're with me all the time, the light and the dark. The loved and the lost.

We're going to be okay. I know it.

THE END

Acknowledgements

No matter how many books I write, the process never gets easier. There are always these moments in which I think to myself: Self, this is the book that breaks me.

But, fortunately, I have an incredible team behind me: my lovely editor, Charlotte Ledger—thank you for your enthusiasm and support. You always know what a story needs to make it better, and this book wouldn't have made it across the finish line without your help. Thank you to Emily Ruston for your brilliant editing and sharp eye.

To the entire team at One More Chapter and HarperCollins for your help. Especially Bethan Morgan and Claire Fenby, for your tireless work behind the scenes (and in front of the scenes), connecting my books with the readers who enjoy them.

I owe a huge thanks to my agent, Katie Shea Boutillier. The day she came on board to be my agent changed my life forever. Her guidance and support have helped make me a better writer, and I wouldn't be where I am without her tireless work and determination. Katie, you're the G.O.A.T.!

To Shannon, Tristian, Dexter, and Violet: for being the loves of my life, and for believing in me even when I don't believe in myself. Love you.